ROUGHING

ROUGHING

Lorna Schultz Nicholson

James Lorimer & Company Ltd., Publishers
Toronto

James Lorimer & Company Ltd., Publishers acknowledges the support of the
Ontario Arts Council. We acknowledge the financial support of the Government
of Canada through the Canada Book Fund for our publishing activities. We
acknowledge the support of the Canada Council for the Arts, which last
year invested $20.1 million in writing and publishing throughout Canada.
We acknowledge the Government of Ontario through the Ontario Media
Development Corporation's Ontario Book Initiative.

Cover photo: iStockophoto

Library and Archives Canada Cataloguing in Publication

Schultz Nicholson, Lorna
        Roughing / by Lorna Schultz Nicholson.

(Sports stories)
Issued also in an electronic format.
ISBN 978-1-55277-567-7

        I. Title. II. Series: Sports stories (Toronto, Ont.)

PS8637.C58R69 2010   jC813'.6   C2010-903313-2

James Lorimer & Company Ltd.,	Distributed in the United States by:
Publishers	Orca Book Publishers
317 Adelaide Street West, Suite 1002	P.O. Box 468
Toronto, ON, Canada	Custer, WA USA
M5V 1P9	98240-0468
www.lorimer.ca	

Printed and bound in Canada.
Manufactured by Friesens Corporation in Altona, Manitoba, Canada in July 2011.
Job # 67255

CONTENTS

To Mandi, Marijean, and Grant

1 INVITATION

Josh Watson woke up and jumped out of bed. Today was the big day!

His hockey team, the Springland Stingers, was playing the third game in a best-of-three series against the Northwest Rockies. The team that won today would be city champions.

Dressed only in boxer shorts, Josh flexed in front of the mirror. The winning team got to skate around the ice carrying the trophy—just like Stanley Cup champions. How heavy was that trophy, anyway? Josh tried to stand tall. He'd gained back the weight he had lost last fall, but he still hadn't grown much in height. Today, he didn't care about any of that. His team was in the championship!

★★★

The whistle blew to start the game. At the bench, Josh's team gathered in their huddle for a big cheer. Josh skated to his position on right wing. He'd been put on the first line. Eric, the team captain, was playing centre and Kaleigh was on left wing. She was one of the best PeeWee hockey players in all of Calgary.

The season had started badly for Josh. No matter how hard he had tried, his play wasn't up to his usual level. And he had been tired and thirsty all the time. He had actually pushed himself until he passed out before he had been diagnosed with type 1 diabetes. But now he had his diabetes regulated, and a winter of practising on his outdoor rink and playing on this top team had really improved his play. Here he was in the final game of the year—on the first line!

The puck dropped and Eric managed to get it on the tip of his stick. He made a weak pass over to Josh. Josh held it on his stick, looked up, and nailed a pass to Kaleigh. She received the pass and took off down the ice, with Eric and Josh speeding behind her.

Kaleigh flipped a pass to Eric, who breezed over the blue line. Josh skated to open ice, hoping to get a pass from Eric or a rebound. The Rockies' defenceman—at least a head taller than Josh—tried to tie him up. Josh kept circling, moving his feet to stay open. The guy stayed on him, relentlessly pushing and shoving to get Josh out of the way. But Josh held his ground.

Kaleigh skated behind the net. She picked up the pass Eric sent her but was stick-checked. Josh raced to the loose puck but got squished into the boards. Kaleigh rushed in for support and there was another scramble. Back on his feet, Josh kept digging until he had the puck on his stick. He felt a shoulder shove him and he started to fall forward. Determined, he reached out and swatted at the puck, hoping it would end up somewhere in front of the net. Just as he made the connection, a body landed on top of him.

From under the Rockies player, Josh heard the people in the arena yelling and...cheering! Lying on the ice, he looked up and grinned. The Rockies' goalie was on the ground and the puck was in the net. Eric had scored!

Josh jumped up and raced over to Eric, who was down on one knee doing the classic victory cheer.

"Awesome pass, Josh." Eric stood up as Josh and the rest of the Stingers skated into a group hug.

They skated to the bench for the line change, and Coach Jim patted their helmets. "That's the way to dig, guys! Let's keep it up."

"That was amazing, Josh," exclaimed Kaleigh. "We scored first shift! Next time out, let's get another goal."

"I just passed it out front, hoping someone could get it." Josh grabbed the pop that he had stashed behind the bench and took a swig.

"Eric one-timed it," said Kaleigh. "But you set it up."

Josh snapped his face cage back on. "We can win this." He hit the boards with his hands. "We need another goal!"

But there were no more goals for either team in

the first period. Or in the second period. And with just one minute of play left in the third period, the score was still 1–0.

On the bench, Josh kept watching the clock. They needed to hold off the Rockies just a little longer, and the city championship would be theirs.

Suddenly, there was a turnover and the best player on the Rockies had a breakaway. He sped toward Sam, who looked very alone in the Stingers' net.

"Come on, Sam," whispered Kaleigh. "You can do it."

Josh didn't say anything, he just watched the action. The Rockies' forward looked as if he was going to make a wrist shot, and Sam got into his crouch, but then the forward made a fake move and pushed the puck to the side. Sam stretched out his leg to try to cover the net, but the Rockies' star player jabbed the puck under Sam's pads. Sam fell back, trying to save the goal, but…the referee made the motion. The puck was in. The Rockies had tied the game.

"Eric, your line's out!"

"Come on, Josh, it's up to us. Remember our face-off play." Kaleigh stepped on the ice just behind Josh. They skated to their wings.

Josh sucked in a deep breath. He glanced at the clock. Forty seconds left.

The puck dropped. Josh skated up his wing, hoping for a breakout pass, but there was a scramble so he circled back. The play only worked if the centre could win the faceoff. Eric struggled for control and swatted it back, but not hard enough to get it to the defence. Fortunately, Kaleigh swept in and picked up the puck. Josh rushed up his wing again, and tapped the ice with his stick. Josh received Kaleigh's pass and sailed over the blue line. He was blocked by the Rockies' defence, so he drop-passed the puck to Eric. Eric kicked it with his skate to get control, but the opposition was all over him. He batted the puck to open ice, where Kaleigh managed to pick it up.

Josh skated, trying to stay open, but Kaleigh just couldn't hang on to the puck. Both teams jabbed and poked with their sticks, trying to get possession.

Then, the puck was loose! Josh made a dive for it, reaching out with his stick. With his hands on the end of his stick, he swung at the puck. The action in front of the goal screened the goalie. Somehow, the puck slid under the goalie's stick and across the line!

The buzzer sounded.

Kaleigh jumped on Josh. "You did it, Josh! You scored the winning goal!" All of a sudden, Josh felt the entire team on top of him. They were all laughing and screaming.

★★★

All smiles, and clutching his trophy, Josh ran out of the dressing room to find his parents. He couldn't wait to see how happy his dad would be.

"Josh, slow down," said Coach Jim, grinning. "I want to talk to you for a minute." He patted Josh on the back. "Great game."

"Thanks." Josh beamed.

Coach Jim pulled a brochure and what looked like a registration form out of his pocket. "You'll have to talk to your parents about this. And I'll talk to them too if you'd like. There's an Elite Hockey Camp in the summer that I think would be good for you."

"Elite Hockey Camp?" Josh's eyes widened. He'd heard everyone talking about the camp, but he never thought he'd be picked to go. "Me?"

"To be honest with you, Josh, I asked Eric first. But he's going to be in Europe with his family during that week. Their trip has been planned for months. So, you're my next best choice." Coach Jim paused. "You've worked hard this year, Josh, and you've overcome a lot of obstacles. I want to reward that dedication and hard work."

Josh felt his legs shaking. He couldn't believe he was being asked to go to an Elite camp. "Is…is anyone else from our team going?"

"Sam will be there," said Coach Jim. "I was only allowed to pick two players. Now, it's an overnight camp, and I'm not sure how your parents feel about you being gone for a week. In the end, of course, it's their decision." Coach Jim handed Josh the brochure and the form.

"They'll let me go. They have to let me go!"

2 REGISTRATION: THREE MONTHS LATER

From the kitchen downstairs, Josh could smell…something. What was his mom cooking? He threw on a pair of sweatpants and a T-shirt and ran down the stairs, jumping the last three steps.

"Josh, you're up early," said his mom when he entered the kitchen.

"I couldn't sleep."

His mother smiled at him. "You're excited?"

"Ye-ah! What's for breakfast?"

"Waffles with fruit salad and bacon. Have you checked your blood sugar?" She cut a melon in half.

"Not yet."

"Well, you'd better get that done so we know how much insulin you should get. You're probably going to be expending quite a bit of energy today." She looked up and winked.

Josh ran back up to his room and pricked his finger to obtain a drop of blood. His blood sugar meter showed that his reading was kind of high for morning, but sometimes when he was excited the adrenaline pushed it up.

His mother fixed his insulin dosage and Josh gave himself the needle. When he'd first found out he had diabetes, the needle sort of freaked him out, and he had his mom inject him. But now, he preferred to do it himself.

"If you have breakfast now you should be okay until registration," said his mom as she mixed the waffle batter. "Just to be safe though—"

"I know," said Josh. "I'll take snacks with me. When are we leaving?"

"In about an hour. Is your bag—"

"Packed and ready to go."

★★★

Josh ducked, hoping no one had seen his mother trying to kiss his forehead. "I'm going to be fine, Mom."

"If you have any problems at all, make sure you tell your coach and phone us right away. I've given everyone our phone numbers." Mrs. Watson lifted Josh's chin with her finger. "I'll have my cell on at all times."

"Mo-o-m," Josh muttered through clenched teeth. "It's just one week. I know what to do, okay?" Parents and players were milling around, and Josh looked through the crowd hoping to spot Sam. When he saw him he waved and bellowed, "Sam!"

"Hey, Josh," Sam yelled from across the lawn, running over. "Hi, Mr. and Mrs. Watson," he said before smacking Josh with a high-five.

"Did you see the list of coaches?" Sam asked. "I got the best goalie coach alive. He used to be in the NHL. I bet I'll learn a ton." Sam mimed making a glove-hand save.

"The skater coaches are amazing too. Some are from the Olympics!" Josh, like Sam, was pumped for the chance to fill the next week with hockey. They would be rooming at the University of Calgary and playing across the street at the Olympic-sized Father David Bauer Arena. The Hockey Canada offices were housed in the same building as the rink. The dressing rooms had built-in lockers with hooks for their jerseys and equipment.

"This is going to be so awesome," said Sam.

"Stuart Green is here," exclaimed Josh.

"He coaches Anaheim now. Who's your roommate?" Sam pulled a crumpled registration form out of his back pocket. "I got that guy from Kelowna. The one we watched on TV."

"You're joking, right? You got Kevin Jennings?" Josh quickly turned back to his parents. "Where's my sheet?"

"Your roommate won't be on it." Sam thrust his form in his back pocket again. "That's just the schedule. The roommate list is in the Red Room, where we registered. They just posted it. I can't believe we're sleeping in dorms." Sam punched the air with his fist. "This is going to be so fun. Come on. Let's go see."

"I've got your schedule, Josh." Mr. Watson handed it to Josh then rumpled his hair. "Have a great time, son. I'm proud of you. Make sure you take care of yourself." Mr. Watson winked. "And have some fun too, would ya?"

"Don't you worry, Mr. Watson," Sam said. "I'll make sure of that."

"Yeah, don't worry, Dad." Josh grinned.

"Are you sure you don't want us to walk to your room with you? Help with your suitcase? Meet your roommate?" his mother asked.

"He can go on his own," said Mr. Watson. "Anyway, Mom, you've already checked this entire place out *and* given your approval. Don't we have some errands to run?"

"Okay, I get it," said Josh's mom. "It's time for me to make my exit." She forced a smile even though her eyes shone with tears. "Have fun, honey. And don't forget—"

"I know, be careful. I will, don't worry. Gotta go. Love you both. See you in a week." Josh faced Sam. "Beat you there!"

Josh and Sam sprinted across the grass and sidewalks to get to the entrance. From there they could walk through underground tunnels to their dorms. The entire university had tunnels so the students could walk anywhere without ever going outside. Of course, that didn't matter much in the summer, only in the cold of winter. But still, it would be kind of fun.

As Sam and Josh rushed into the Red Room, they immediately saw the bulletin board surrounded by a bunch of guys. Everyone was talking—the buzz was almost deafening. Josh pushed his way into the crowd to get a look at the board. Sam was right on his heels.

"It looks like I'm with a guy from the Northwest Territories." Josh pointed to the listing for room 21. Beside the room number was his name and where he was from, and the name of his roommate and where he was from. "Peter Kuiksak from Tuktoyaktuk," said Josh with difficulty. "That's a mouthful."

"Must be up in the boonies," said Sam.

"I wonder if he's any good."

"Everyone at this camp is good." Sam punched Josh's arm. "That's why we got picked." Sam pointed to his room listing: 28. "I'm just down the hall from you."

"Let's go unpack," said Josh.

Josh and Sam pushed through the crowd—which had thinned a bit—until they were in the clear. Josh spotted his suitcase, sitting exactly where his dad had left it when they'd first registered. Fifteen minutes ago, there had been a big pile of suitcases, now his was one of a few. Everyone must be in their rooms already. He raced over, pulled out the handle of his case, and wheeled it over to Sam.

"I'm ready." He pointed down the stairs. "That way, I guess."

"Yep," said Sam. "Our new home for a whole week. Yeaaah!"

Josh high-fived Sam again. One week at camp with no parents, no big brother or little sister, and a whole lot of hockey. Josh and Sam rushed down the stairs and through a door that led into a big lobby. Then they moved in the direction of the sign that said *Kananaskis Hall*.

Josh hurried down the tunnel, moving so fast that his suitcase teetered on one wheel. He couldn't wait for camp to officially start. He would be sleeping in a university dorm, and eating in the university cafeteria. Players had ice time twice daily for a total of three hours, and there would be extensive dry-land training. The down time was filled with motivational seminars, video viewings, and creative visualization. Also included was a trip to Banff on Wednesday.

"How cool is it that, that our hockey equipment is already over at the arena? And that our names are above those cubbies?" Sam asked Josh, panting.

"I've got my equipment hanging there already," said Josh.

At the entrance to room 21, Josh stopped. "I guess I'll see you at the meeting. If you get there first, save me a seat." He paused. "Hey, don't tell anyone I've got diabetes, okay?"

"What difference does it make? No one will care."

Josh shrugged. "I just don't want anyone to know."

"Whatever." Sam looked at his watch. "We don't have much time. The first meeting starts in, like, a half hour. I'd better get moving. I've got undies to unpack."

Josh laughed. "Clean ones, I hope."

3 ROOMMATE

When Josh entered his dorm room, he was disappointed to discover that he was alone. From the lack of stuff, he could see that his roommate hadn't even arrived yet. For a minute or so, Josh stood in the centre of the room to assess the situation. The space wasn't huge, that was for sure. In fact, it was about the size of his bedroom at home. The room contained two beds, two desks, and two night tables. There were doors to two closets. The beds sat on either side of the room and there was a little space between them.

Josh untied his sleeping bag and pillow and threw them on the bed closest to the door. The washrooms were located down the hall and, even though it had not been a problem for a while, sometimes if his blood sugar was high he had to go in the middle of the night. Might as well avoid tripping over his roommate's bed if he had to go.

Next, Josh opened his suitcase and took out all his clothes—clean boxers included. He stacked and hung everything in the closet closest to his bed.

After putting away his clothes, Josh pulled out the few pictures he had brought. One was of him and Kaleigh carrying the City Championsips trophy around the ice, the photo Kaleigh had got framed for Josh's thirteenth birthday in June. The only other snap-shot he had was a family photo his little sister Amy had given to him as a going-away gift, and it was in a frame she had made herself out of shells. He had to smile when he set the photo on the night table. Amy usually annoyed Josh…except when she did things like snuggle up with him on the couch or secretly make him a present. Then she was alright.

On the bottom of Josh's suitcase, in a shoe box, were the extra snacks his mom had packed to prevent low blood sugar. He searched the room for a place where he could hide the stuff, wondering what this unknown Peter guy would think if he happened to find out Josh had diabetes. Would he be grossed out?

Josh hoped no one would find out. He didn't want to be different. How could he hide it from his room-mate? Josh decided the best place for the snack box was in his night table. He jammed it in the bottom shelf and shut the door.

All Josh's diabetes paraphernalia was packed in a nondescript black shaving kit that his mom had bought for him at the drug store. She'd organized his insu-lin pens, blood monitoring kit, and sugar tablets, and gone over everything with Josh about a zillion times. Josh shook his head when he saw her calligraphy-style handwriting on a piece of paper.

Josh sped through the incredibly long two-page note, sticking it the pocket of his suitcase when he was done. No doubt about it, his mom was worried. But he knew nothing was going to go wrong.

He glanced at his miniature clock radio and realized he had ten minutes before he had to be at the meeting. He *should* check his blood glucose. If Mom hadn't written that note, he might have forgotten.

Josh checked the hallway and, when he didn't see anyone, he half shut the door to the room and ran back to his bed. He quickly pricked his finger and administered the test—he was shocked his reading was so high. But then he hadn't exercised yet, and he'd had a big lunch, and he was excited for camp to begin. Josh looked at the schedule. Tonight it said, *Light Skate*.

Josh rubbed the sweat off his forehead. Should he ride this out? He didn't know if the practice would be hard enough to lower his blood sugar level. Josh closed his eyes to think.

A few seconds later—he had to hurry—he pulled out his insulin pen and filled it with an insulin cartridge. Josh felt funny, giving himself an injection in this room. Should he go to the bathroom? He really only needed a few seconds. Grabbing a handful of flesh on his leg, he jabbed the pen in, counting to five before pulling it out.

What did Mom say in her note? Josh grimaced when he remembered. He wasn't supposed to use his thigh for the injection. The doctor had said that he should always inject into his abdomen before playing hockey, because it was the least exercised area. He'd practised at the diabetes clinic, injecting in his abdomen—how could he have forgotten already?

Suddenly, Josh heard a raspy cough. He looked up to see a thickly built boy with dark black hair and toffee-coloured skin standing at the doorway, an old canvas duffle bag slung over his shoulder. Josh hadn't heard him open the door. Had he been watching Josh?

Josh hid the pen behind his back. The boy didn't say a word as he walked into the room, but he did have a puzzled look on his face.

"I'm Josh." Josh sat tall on the end of his bed. His throat was dry and his palms were sweaty. Would the guy think he was a drug addict or into steroids?

Josh's roommate nodded but didn't say anything.

"I hope, um, that it's okay with you that I, uh, took this bed?"

The guy shrugged as he looked at both beds. Then he turned and dropped his bag on the floor. Josh stood up, his insulin pen held tightly in his fist behind his back.

"We each have our own closet," said Josh, pointing to the closet closest to the other bed. "You can put your stuff in there." His voice sounded high and forced.

The guy unzipped his bag and pulled out T-shirts, shorts, socks, and underwear.

For a few seconds, Josh watched this roommate shove his clothes in the closet. What was it going to be like living with this guy for one week? He hadn't even introduced himself. Or said one word. Josh's stomach did flip-flops. Maybe his roommate did see the injection and thought Josh was doing something illegal. Should Josh say something about his diabetes? Josh was relieved when he looked at his watch and saw that there was only five minutes before the debriefing session.

"Hey, um, I'm going to head to the meeting. I think it's in that Red Room, where we registered. I'll see you there, okay?"

The roommate nodded.

Josh turned his back, quickly disassembled his pen, shoved it in his black kit, and headed for the door.

"You have diabetes?" The voice was low, almost monotone.

"Ye-ah." Josh stopped and turned. "Um, don't…tell anyone else, okay?"

"My mom had it too," said the roommate, without looking up.

"Oh," said Josh, bewildered but relieved.

The roommate gestured to the black kit where Josh had put his needle. "She had to do that."

"You mean injections?" Josh didn't know what to say. He probably sounded like a complete nerd.

Roommate

"Not no more though." The roommate still avoided eye contact with Josh.

Josh rocked back and forth on his heels. To be polite, should he keep talking? He'd never heard of anyone with type 1 diabetes who didn't need insulin injections. "How'd she…uh…get so she didn't, uh, have to, you know, inject insulin anymore?" Now Josh was sounding like a boring medical textbook.

"She died."

4 BIG SURPRISE

At the debriefing meeting, Josh saw Sam sitting near the front. Was he with Kevin Jennings? Sam waved to Josh and pointed to the empty seat he had saved. Josh wove his way around the chairs.

"Josh," Sam said standing, puffing out his chest, "meet my roommate, Kevin."

"Hi," said Josh, swallowing, hoping he sounded cool. What else should he say? Should he talk about hockey? Tell Kevin that he was good? Kevin was the best thirteen-year-old hockey player in all of Canada. Everyone in the country was watching his progress. Last spring, The Sports Network had even done a ten-minute segment on him. Lucky Sam was rooming with a *celebrity*.

Kevin stayed slouched in his seat and lifted his hand to give a small wave. Josh wanted to talk, but no words came out, so he just waved back and shoved his hands in his pockets.

Sam asked Josh, "So where's your roommate?"

"Unpacking." Josh glanced around the room. "He'll

be late if he doesn't get here soon. But, hey, it's not my problem." Feeling as if he was rambling, Josh sat down.

Kevin leaned forward with his elbows on his knees. "What's the guy's name?"

"Peter something or other. He's from the North," replied Josh.

"Are you with Peter Kuiksak?"

"Yeah, that's him."

"Have you ever seen him play?"

"Never."

"Neither have I. I've heard he's a total—"

A voice boomed from the front, interrupting Kevin. Although he wanted to hear more about his roommate, Josh gave his full attention to the front of the room.

"Welcome to camp!" A tall and burly man stood there, wearing a black track suit with *Elite Summer Hockey Camp* embroidered on the front. "My name is Stuart Green, but for this week, call me Coach Green." Everyone in the room broke into loud cheers. Stuart Green was a NHL legend and last year had coached the Canadian Junior Team to gold at the World Championships. Josh could hardly believe he was actually going to be on the ice with him.

Coach Green raised his arms to stop the noise. When the room had hushed he continued. "Everyone in this room has been selected for this camp because of the successful year you just finished." He paused to look around the room at the thirty boys. "Congratulations!"

The room erupted again. Smiling, Coach Green raised his arms again to stop the hooting and hollering.

"In this room right now," he said, in a powerful, mesmerizing voice, "is tremendous talent. We're hoping that after one week, every one of you will see a noticeable change in your skills. Of course, you're all working on different aspects of the game, so make sure you stay focused on the goals that you, as an individual, want to accomplish. And it is a terrific game, isn't it boys? We all love hockey, right?!"

"Yeah! Yeah!" Josh felt the adrenaline rushing through his body. This had to be the most exciting moment in his hockey career so far.

After quieting the crowd, Coach Green continued, "That's the enthusiasm we want to see for the entire week. We do expect a lot from each and every one of you, and that includes being prepared both mentally and physically for every session—dry-land and ice. No ifs, ands, or buts. And if there are any behaviour problems, you'll be sent home immediately. Alcohol and drugs are prohibited. Curfew is curfew. Tardiness is unacceptable."

Coach Green looked at his watch. "Okay, hockey players, because we can't be late for our first ice session—which is in less than an hour—I want to quickly go over the rules and regulations regarding this camp. And I want to introduce our coaching staff."

One by one the rules were stated—no roaming the campus; no roaming the arena or Hockey Canada office; all players when not skating or at dry-land sessions were to stay in the housing area. Josh listened as Coach Green listed at least twenty rules. Then the rest of the coaching staff stood to be introduced to the players.

In less than fifteen minutes, Josh was walking down the path beside Sam and Kevin toward the rink across the street. The sun glistened in the summer sky, warming his skin. The hot breeze flushed his face and he felt as if he was in another world. Was he really at this Elite Hockey Camp?

When they were off the university grounds and on the city street that led to the rink, Josh saw a sign with the red and black *Hockey Canada* emblem and the words Hockey Canada. His skin tingled with excitement. Sometimes the Olympic teams held their camps here.

Once in the arena, Josh ended up in the same dressing room as Sam and Kevin. In record time he was dressed. He wanted to be out in the hall, ready to go on the ice as soon as the Zamboni was finishing its last round.

Bent over, tying his laces, Josh heard the dressing-room door open. Fully expecting a coach, Josh was surprised when he saw Peter. Didn't he know that being late was unacceptable? No one said a word to Peter as he crossed the room, stepping over shoes, to find his gear. Josh glanced at Sam and shrugged his shoulders. In return, Sam scrunched up his face and shook his head. Sam was already completely dressed, goal pads and all, and Peter didn't even have a shin pad on yet.

Kevin leaned over and whispered to Sam and Josh, "Can you believe how late the guy is? He doesn't deserve to be at this camp." Kevin stood and clicked his face cage onto his helmet. Ready, he headed to the door, picking up his stick on the way. Josh resumed tying his skates—he wanted to be the next player out the door.

★★★

On the ice, Josh lunged to stretch his groin and legs. Then he put his stick on his shoulders to stretch out his back so he would be good and loose before drills started. Just as the whistle blew, Josh saw Peter step on the ice and skate over to where the coaches were standing by the white board. The guy hadn't warmed up at all.

In the circle, Josh tried to get beside Kevin, but he ended up next to Peter. Peter's equipment looked older, used. His pants sported holes, as did his socks, and his skates were an old Bauer model. Josh was sure that Bauer didn't even make that kind of skate anymore. The guy must have gotten them from a secondhand sale. Josh was wearing the brand-new Graf custom skates his parents had bought him for his birthday.

Peter didn't acknowledge Josh's presence, so Josh

faced the front. Coach Green was using felt marker to draw the first skating drill—stops and starts at the corners of every line. Keeping heads up was important as a line was going from either end. Josh had done this drill a million times, so when Coach Green blew the whistle, he raced to be first in line. Kevin headed up the line on the other side of the rink. Josh noticed that Peter was at the tail end of Kevin's line. What was with that guy? Maybe he wasn't any good and was at the camp because someone had offered to pay for his week.

The whistle blew and Josh took off in a crouch. He stopped and started at each corner, first one way then the next. His edges felt good and sharp—his new skates were light and they fit tight.

When he finished zig-zagging across the big Olympic ice surface, he bent over at the waist for a minute. The extra width of the rink sure made a difference. After catching his breath, he headed to the back of the line. The "light skate" on this big rink might not be so light.

From his end, Josh could see the guys on the opposite side. Kevin, like Josh, was finished and waiting. He stood behind Peter. Finally, both lines were on their last player. Peter got in his ready position. Josh hoped his roommate would be able to skate half decently, although in those skates that could be tough. Josh saw Kevin nonchalantly put his stick under Peter's skates. None of the coaches noticed. Peter stumbled, but quickly recovered by kicking Kevin's stick so hard it flew out of his hands. Then he took off.

Josh's eyes widened and he held his breath. The guy was quick. And when he stopped, he sprayed ice everywhere. Mesmerized, Josh watched Peter's powerful transition from a stop to a start. Josh knew Peter would outskate him any day.

Although Peter started from behind, he crossed his line first.

5 STRENGTHS AND WEAKNESSES

Josh learned in the first ice session that Kevin wasn't the only star on the ice. Peter was as fast, if not faster than Kevin. And could he shoot the puck! His slapshot, even from the blue line, could ping the crossbar. Even though Sam tried, he only managed to glove save one of Peter's shots. All the others whizzed past him into the back of the net. Josh figured Peter must have arms the size of telephone poles.

They had just finished a skating and passing drill, weaving down the length of the ice, when Coach Green blew the whistle. Josh hustled to the white board and got down on one knee. This first ice session had worked on skating, passing, and shooting. Josh felt he was keeping up as far as skating and passing went, but his size kept him from having real power in his shots. There were smaller players in the NHL and they scored with finesse instead of strength. Maybe there was hope for Josh yet.

"So far, so good, guys," Coach Green addressed the

group. "For the last thirty minutes of this session, I'm going to divide you into four groups and you'll rotate around the corners. At least two coaches will be at each station to give you individual help. Remember, tomorrow night we're going to meet with each of you to talk about your specific goals for this camp—what part of your game you want to improve. You need to think seriously about this and come to the meeting prepared."

He pointed to the board to show the boys the drills. In one corner was a shooting drill where the coach would help each player with the actual mechanics of his shot. Another corner would work on passing, another on agility, and finally there was a corner on checking. Josh knew the checking would be the killer for him— some of these guys were huge.

Coach Green gave everyone a number between one and four to split them into four groups, and Josh ended up in the same group as Kevin. Thankful that they had passing first, Josh started to skate to his assigned corner.

Kevin skated up beside Josh and said, "I wish I was in hitting. I'd like to be partnered with that guy." He pointed to Peter, who was heading over to the hitting station. "I'd show him what it's like to take a real check. He thinks he plays tough-guy hockey, but he doesn't."

This kind of talk about hitting was totally out of Josh's league so he didn't answer. Instead, he picked up a puck. Nervous about asking Kevin to be his partner, in case he messed up, Josh turned to another player.

"I'll partner with you."

"Sure." The guy nodded and they moved away from each other. They were told to pass the puck on the skates instead of the stick, to learn how to kick it to the stick then make a quick pass. This was the kind of drill Josh liked and was good at. Last winter, Josh had spent hours on his outdoor rink with his big brother, Matt, practising moving the puck in his skates. Matt had told Josh it was an important skill.

When the whistle blew, Josh moved to the shooting station. The coach explained to Josh all about transferring his weight to make a decent wrist shot, and encouraged him to continue using his wrist shot until he got a bit bigger. After all, the coach reminded Josh, Walter Gretzky only let Wayne use a slapshot after he'd put on some weight and muscle...and that was when he was ready to play with the Juniors!

The coach did show Josh the proper mechanics of the slapshot, how to lean in and follow through. He told Josh to keep practising. Josh couldn't believe how much he improved in just one session with the shooting coach!

At the next station, Josh went through a number of agility exercises. He loved jumping over sticks and skating around cones to practise tight turns. In this drill, being small helped him.

By the time Josh got to his last station—hitting— he was starting to feel weak. Had he given himself too much insulin, causing his blood sugar to go too low?

The practice had been more than a light skate. Josh checked the clock. Five minutes to go.

Kevin skated up to Josh and asked him to be his partner. Josh couldn't believe it. One player was to set up along the boards with the puck. The other player was to check the one with the puck.

To delay being the one to actually take the hit, Josh slapped a puck to Kevin, who lined up at the blue line. When Kevin took off down the boards, Josh took a deep breath and skated at full speed, thrusting into him shoulder-first. The hit had little impact; Kevin remained standing and still had possession of the puck. Josh figured he'd better write down checking as his number-one thing to work on.

When it was Josh's turn, he squared off at the blue line. As he stickhandled down the boards, he kept his head up, looking for Kevin. Seeing him close, Josh made a quick turn and scooted around Kevin. Kevin smashed into the boards and Josh still had possession of the puck.

"Good job," said Coach Hal to Josh. Then he turned to Kevin and said, "Kevin, anticipate. Read your opponent and be one step ahead."

"I'll get you next time," said Kevin under his breath.

With only three minutes left in the practice, Josh hoped that they wouldn't have to do the drill again. He winced, thinking of Kevin coming at him. Unfortunately, when it was Josh's turn at the blue line, there was still a minute left.

Josh cradled the puck on his stick, waiting for the go-ahead. When he heard the whistle, he sucked in a deep breath and skated. He saw and heard Kevin coming toward him and, although he knew he should outsmart Kevin and try a different move, he panicked. This time, Kevin read him well. Josh got nailed. He crashed to the ice in one big swoop.

"Told you I'd get you good," Kevin laughed as the whistle blew to end practice.

"Yeah, you got me all right." Josh shook his head to get rid of the stars in his eyes. He was thankful the practice was over.

★★★

In the dressing room, Josh unzipped the outer pocket of his bag and pulled out a pop. He quickly opened it and, without even letting the fizz settle, downed half of it. Then he sat back and wiped his mouth. Right away, he could feel the drink help raise his sugar level, but he knew he should follow up with some kind of snack. Josh hadn't brought crackers with him. They always got smashed up.

"I can't believe you're drinking pop after practice," Kevin said, frowning at Josh.

"I, uh, pressed the wrong button on the machine," mumbled Josh. "I didn't want to waste my money." He started untying his skates.

He had his head down when he heard Kevin call out, "Hey, Eskimo boy."

Everyone knew who Kevin was talking to. As Josh tugged at his lace, he peered at Peter. All he could see was Peter's dark hair as he leaned over the skates he was taking off.

Kevin continued, "Wish we were together in the hitting drill. I could have shown you a thing or two."

Peter yanked his skate off and wiped it with a cloth.

Kevin rolled up his used sock tape and threw it in Peter's direction. Peter dodged the tape without looking at Kevin.

6 ICEBREAKER

The cafeteria was located by the Olympic Oval. Josh was hungry from the practice, and he desperately needed more food after his low blood sugar. He entered the cafeteria, so deep in thought about what to eat and what not to eat that he accidentally bumped into Peter.

"Sorry," he mumbled.

"It's okay," replied Peter.

"What's for dinner?" Josh asked.

Peter shrugged. "Probably spaghetti and bread."

"Good," said Josh relieved. Carbohydrates.

"Hey, Josh!" Josh found Sam, who was waving like a madman. "Over here!"

Josh turned back to Peter. "See ya later."

Peter pivoted and walked toward the food line.

As Josh approached the round table where Sam, Kevin, and a few of the other guys were sitting, he said, "I'm starving, let's get in line."

"Good idea." Kevin jumped over his chair.

All the guys at the table leaped up and ran to get in

line, knocking over chairs on the way. Kevin managed to be first. Josh was next.

"Great practice, eh?" Josh stood ahead of Sam.

Sam's eyes widened. "I could hardly stop your roommate's shot. The one time I did, it blistered my hand. No one in our league shoots like that."

The guys must have heard Sam's comment. One of them said, "He can hit too. He's made of cement."

"Watch this." Kevin stepped out of his place to move up the line. He got to Peter, who was almost at the front of the line, and pointed to Peter's shoe. "Hey, your lace is untied."

When Peter glanced down at his shoe, Kevin knocked his ball cap off his head. Peter immediately stepped out of line to pick up his cap. Kevin zipped into the line in front of Peter.

"Thanks for the spot," said Kevin, playfully slapping Peter on the back. "I one-upped you." Grinning, Kevin peered at the back of the line, giving Sam and Josh and all the other guys the thumbs-up. Everyone laughed but Josh—he was too busy thinking about dinner.

★★★

The spaghetti tasted absolutely awesome. Josh hunkered down to devour everything on his plate—salad included—plus two pieces of bread. Only once did he look up, and he saw Peter sitting all by himself three tables over. As soon as their eyes caught, Peter lowered his head. So did Josh—to finish his meal. Josh needed to think about eating and not the fact that his roommate was alone.

After dinner, everyone was to meet in the Red Room for an icebreaking session. Feeling great with food in his body, Josh practically ran up the stairs. This was going to be fun. He'd met Rory and Nelson at dinner—they were friends of Kevin's from Toronto—but he didn't know many of the other guys yet. Josh couldn't believe there were guys at camp from so far away.

As he entered the room, he was greeted by Coach Green, who handed him a name tag and felt marker. "First name, okay?"

A guy behind Josh asked, "How about nicknames?"

Coach Green raised his eyebrows. "They've got to be decent."

Josh wrote his real name on his name tag and stuck it to his shirt. He saw Sam, Kevin, Nelson, and Rory over by the windows, and noticed Peter sitting by himself again. The guy was so quiet that Josh was sure this kind of initiation wasn't his thing.

Once the entire group was sitting down, the coaches stood at the front of the room and told everyone to get into pairs with a person they didn't know. They were to find out a few interesting things so they could introduce that person. A red-haired guy two seats over nabbed Josh.

"I'll go with you." His name tag said Mike.

"Sure."

Josh turned his chair so they were facing each other. "Where are you from?" he asked.

"Regina. How about you?"

"Calgary." Josh paused. This exercise was hard. What was he supposed to ask Mike now? "Um. Do you have a big family?"

"One little brother. You?"

"I have an older brother, Matt, and a little sister named Amy."

Mike nodded. They both remained silent until Mike asked, "What's your favourite sport?" Immediately following his question he laughed. "What a dumb question."

"Ringette," Josh joked.

Mike rolled his eyes. Then he grinned. "I got one. Who's your favourite girl?"

Josh grinned. "Ah, let's see. *My mother*," said Josh, batting his eyelashes and looking all sweet and innocent. "Or Kaleigh," he said, dropping the funny act.

"Who's Kaleigh?"

"Kaleigh Radcliffe. She played on our hockey team last year. She wants to be on the Olympic team one day. So what about you? Come on, tell me—who's your favourite girl?"

"Catwoman. She can karate kick."

Josh was about to ask another question when the

coaches announced that time was up, and it was time for the guys to introduce their partners.

Although Josh laughed at some of the things the guys were saying, he also felt a bit nervous. He hated speaking in public.

Finally, they called his name.

"This is Mike," he gestured. "He's from Regina. His favorite sport is hockey."

"Like we didn't know that," someone yelled.

Josh grinned. "Okay, and his favorite girl in the world is Catwoman because she can karate kick."

"All right!" yelled most of the guys. No intro yet had included anything about girls. Josh smiled, proud of himself—he had got the crowd going.

Mike shook his head at Josh, smiling. "You're in for it," he whispered as he stood. "This is Josh, from Calgary. And he wanted to say his favorite girl is…" Mike paused for a second to smile and glance around the room, obviously wanting full attention. Once everyone was anxiously waiting he continued, "…his mom but—"

Everyone booed. Mike grinned.

When everyone quieted down, Mike continued. "His favorite girl is…da-da-dun…" Mike jumped to stand on a chair. Then he yelled, "KALEIGH."

All the guys started chanting, "Kaleigh, Kaleigh."

Josh could feel the heat in his cheeks. This was so embarrassing. His face had to be ten shades of red. Sam was laughing so hard, he was almost choking.

"He got you good," said Sam hysterically, pointing to Josh.

After what seemed like forever to Josh, Coach Green silenced the group and moved on to the next pair. The game continued to have some good laughs. Finally, there was only one pair left—Peter and his partner.

Peter stood. Josh could tell he was super nervous.

"This is Brady," he said quietly.

Kevin leaned over and whispered, "We can't even hear him."

Peter continued. "Um. He's from Manitoba. He likes hockey, he speaks French, and he likes to wake board." Peter eyed the room for a minute, not saying anything. Finally, he shrugged. "Isn't my time up yet?"

Everyone broke into laughter. Kevin slouched in his seat. "That wasn't funny."

"I think it was," whispered Sam. "It's exactly how I felt when it was my turn."

"Yeah, but at least you didn't admit to it."

"Your turn, Brady," said Coach Green holding up his hand.

Brady motioned to Peter. "This is Peter. He's from… ah, he's from a place that I can't pronounce. It has, like, a hundred letters."

For the first time since Josh had met Peter he saw him smile. Peter mouthed, "Tuk-toy-ak-tuk."

"That's it." Brady gave the crowd a thumb's up.

"Bonus. Now I don't have to say it. Peter, here, has four brothers and three sisters. Big family. Oh yeah, and hockey up in that Tuk place is still played on real ice. They don't have any artificial ice like we have. That's it, that's all."

Kevin whispered to Sam, "I've heard that big family of his is weird. I think his mother may have even done herself in."

Josh stared from Kevin to Peter. Could that be true?

7 CONVERSATION

Lights were to be out at eleven. At ten-fifteen Josh headed back to the room. The rest of the guys were going to play one more round of cards, but Josh had to check his blood sugar, give himself his bedtime insulin, and eat a snack. *What a pain*, he thought. He wished he didn't have diabetes.

Peter was lying in his bed, reading, when Josh entered the dorm room. Josh noticed that Peter had set up a few personal things while Josh was out playing cards. A painting of a raven stood on his desk. The black bird was surrounded by bright colours: engine red, lemon yellow, and sea blue. Josh liked it, and was surprised how much it brightened the drab room. On Peter's night stand stood a carving of what looked like a bear. Had Peter carved it himself? A photo of a young girl with a baby on her back caught Josh's attention. He wondered who it was. Then Josh noticed a drum sitting on the floor beside the nightstand. Peter must have had it rolled in his sleeping bag.

"You're back early," said Josh.

"Yeah," Peter mumbled without looking up from his book.

Josh noticed that, even after the icebreaker, Peter still didn't have anyone to hang out with. He had been talking with Brady for a bit, but then Brady had joined another group for cards.

Josh sat on the end of his bed. He was uncomfortable that he had to pull out all his diabetes stuff in front of a guy he hardly knew. He could go into the washroom. But then some of the other guys might find out. He slowly opened the drawer to his nightstand, remembering that Peter had said his mother had diabetes too. Did Peter's mother really kill herself? Leave so many kids? What had Brady said, *four brothers and three sisters*?

His face flushed in embarrassment, Josh pricked his finger. Then he checked his glucose and wrote the level in his record book. He opted to get undressed for bed before giving himself an injection on the off chance that Peter might head to the bathroom, leaving Josh with the room to himself. Or Josh could go hide in one of the bathroom stalls.

Josh knew he had to have some kind of snack, or he'd never make it through the night. He felt like an idiot eating snacks in front of Peter, so when he pulled out his snack bag he asked, "Do you want a granola bar?"

Peter peered up from his book. "Sure."

Josh threw one. Peter caught it in one hand.

"I, uh, your drum is cool." Josh pointed to the drum.

Peter nodded and ripped open the wrapper of the granola bar. He took a bite, chewed, then said, "I brought it in case I have spare time."

"Schedule's tight," said Josh.

"Yeah," replied Peter.

"Do you drum a lot where you come from?"

"I belong to a team. We go in competitions."

"Cool. Is it fun?"

"I wouldn't do it if it wasn't."

"I think Banff will be fun," said Josh, trying to keep the conversation going for a few more minutes.

"I've never been to Banff." Peter finished his granola bar and sat up to try to basketball-toss his wrapper in the garbage.

When he missed, Josh picked it up and did a jump shot, tossing his wrapper and Peter's in the garbage.

"Good shot," said Peter.

"Thanks." Josh glanced at Peter, making eye contact for the first time. "Have you really never been to Banff?"

Peter shook his head.

"I guess it's a lot farther from where you live than it is from Calgary. How'd you get to this camp?"

"Coach Green came to the hamlet where I live last winter and did a talk. He watched me in a tournament in Inuvik. He invited me."

"Do you have a lot of teams up there?" Josh tossed Peter a dried fruit snack.

Peter caught the treat. "Maybe four, if we're lucky. Inuvik, Aklavik, Paulutuk, and Tuk. We play the same teams over and over. It gets really boring."

"Are those places close by your town?" Josh had never met someone from the North before.

"Nah. Sometimes we drive four hours." Peter tore the fruit leather in two. He raised his eyebrows, cracked a smile and said, "It's easier to drive fast on an ice road than slow, though." He shoved half of the fruit snack in his mouth.

Peter had lost Josh. Ice road? "What's an ice road?"

Peter hung his legs over the side of the bed. "A road they make on the river. You know, on ice."

"You don't have real roads?"

"In the hamlet we do. But not to other hamlets. Summer we go by boat, winter the ice road."

"Aren't you afraid you'll crack the ice?"

Peter snorted in laughter. "No," he said.

Josh took out his toothbrush and toothpaste, feeling a bit foolish that he was so ignorant when it came to part of his own country. Did everyone up there play great hockey like Peter? "I bet there are lots of good players where you live," said Josh pulling out a hand towel and picking up his black kit.

"Nope." Peter popped the rest of the snack in his mouth, crumpled up the wrapper and stood to take a jump shot. This time he sunk it. "Some can hardly skate."

"You play with guys who can't skate?" Josh asked shocked.

"Well, they can skate a little but not a lot." Peter went into his nightstand for his toothbrush and tooth-paste.

"You must score a lot of goals."

Peter shrugged, deep in thought. "It's no fun after a while. That's why Coach Green wanted me to come to this camp. He thinks I should move down here. Billet with some family when I'm, like, Midget age. He's been talking to my dad."

"What's your dad say?" What would it be like to have to leave home to play hockey? Josh was lucky; he played in a big city with lots of good players.

"I'll never get anywhere in Tuk," said Peter, heading toward the door. "My dad—he doesn't want me to end up like my two older brothers, getting into trouble all the time." He paused. "Or like my mom," he said softly.

They didn't say another word as they walked down the hall. Josh pushed open the bathroom door and went into one of the stalls. He pulled the toilet seat down so he could sit. His mind whirled as he prepared his insulin pen, trying to absorb everything he'd learned about Peter. He sure lived a different life.

8 CARD GAME

The Monday morning ice session was unbelievably gruelling. When Josh got off the ice his stomach was sick and he felt sweaty—not exercise sweaty, just clammy. His hands were shaking so much he could hardly untie his skates. And he'd forgotten to bring a pop.

"Hey, Josh," said Sam, throwing tape in the garbage can. "I'll walk with you to dry-land."

Josh rubbed his brow. "Yeah, okay."

The dry-land session was being held at the Olympic Oval, in the weight-training area. Josh glanced at his watch. They had a half hour before it started. "I'm going to head to my room for a minute first," he whispered to Sam as he started to undress. "I need food."

"Sure, we got time," said Sam.

Sam and Josh were joined by Kevin, Rory, and Nelson as they walked back. Although Josh's legs felt as weak as watery milkshakes, he tried to act normal to keep up with the rest of the guys.

"Hey, did you hear the joke about the farmer and

the pig?" said Kevin, flicking his soggy hair.

"Watch it," said Sam, ducking. "You just sprayed sweat all over me."

Kevin started shaking his head like a dog. Everyone burst out laughing. Then Kevin proceeded to tell his joke, which made everyone laugh even louder. His pig noises were incredibly funny!

Finally—after what seemed like ages to Josh—they made the pit-stop at Josh's room. Peter wasn't there. Kevin immediately went over to Peter's side of the room.

"What is this?" He picked up Peter's drum.

"What does it look like?" Sam asked sarcastically.

"Why would anyone bring *this* to hockey camp?" Kevin beat the drum and made some loud whooping noises.

Josh rummaged through the snack box in his night-stand. He wondered if he should offer everyone something. It would be the polite thing to do. But then his snacks would dwindle down.

"What do you have in there?" Kevin looked over Josh's shoulder.

"A few things my mom packed." Josh stood. "You want a granola bar?"

"Right on," said Kevin. "I'm starving. I like you, you got food." Kevin shoved the entire granola bar in his mouth and all the guys laughed.

After Josh had doled out a snack to each of the guys and quickly eaten his own snack, they headed over to the Olympic Oval. For the first ten minutes of dry-land training they stretched, getting a bit of a break. Then they got into exercises. They worked with balancing apparatus and rubber tubes for strengthening, and they did all kinds of quick feet exercises. At the end of the session, they played basketball. The entire session was challenging but fun. At the half-way mark, Josh was a little tired. When it was over, he was weak and his body felt floppy.

★★★

In the cafeteria, Josh wolfed down his lunch and immediately felt his energy return. After lunch, they had an hour of down time before they had to head over to the rink for the second ice session. When Josh finally made it outside, he found Sam and a few of the other guys playing the card game Cheat. The gist of the game was to cheat without getting caught. If someone had a bad hand of cards, they could say they had a good hand, but if someone called "cheat," they lost. He sat down on the grass to watch. Sam and Kevin were taking on Rory and Nelson. On the sidelines waiting to play the winners were Graham and Ryan. Josh wanted to play.

"I'll find a partner," said Josh, standing up. "We can play the losers."

"That sounds okay to me." Kevin slapped a card down. "But guaranteed you won't be playing us.

Sammy-boy and I are just too good."

"Just you wait," said Graham. "We'll whup your butts."

"Yeah, right," said Kevin.

"There's Peter." Josh pointed to the other side of the rotunda where Peter sat cross-legged under a tree. "I'll see if he wants to play."

"I wouldn't ask him," said Kevin, staring at the cards in his hand. "He'd be a lousy partner. He's not exactly friendly." Kevin picked up a card. "See the way the guy skates? No finesse at all. He probably plays cards the same way. But, hey, it's your choice."

Josh didn't want to argue with Kevin. But he thought Peter was an amazing hockey player, a bit rough-looking but strong and tough.

Kevin looked at Josh then he made a funny face, pretending to be serious as he studied his cards. Suddenly, Josh knew that Kevin was mimicking him. All the guys laughed, even Josh. Did he really look that serious?

"This game we're playing is for us smart guys." Kevin puffed up his chest and tossed a card down. "See how I did that? I've been practising that move forever."

"You're such a loser," said Rory, laughing as he knocked Kevin's hat off his head.

"Come on, guys, let's finish this game before we have to go to the arena," said Nelson, picking up Kevin's hat and throwing it in the bushes.

Sam picked up two cards before he looked up at

Josh. "Why don't you ask Mike, that guy from Regina? I bet he'd play."

"Yeah, the guy that got you good about *Ka-leigh*," teased Kevin.

Josh glanced around, spotted Mike, and waved to him.

★★★

The card games were only half-way through when the boys had to pack up and leave for the arena. After the afternoon ice session were the individual interviews, then the video analysis in the evening. The guys made a plan to finish the card games in Kevin's room after nine o'clock.

The first half of the afternoon ice session consisted of skating. Peter won every single race. *Does the guy never get tired?* Josh wondered. Sweat seemed to drip from every pore on Josh's body. Even the inside of his ears were wet. As he headed over to the bench for water, he wondered if he should add skating to his list of things he'd like to work on.

Josh stood by the boards squirting water in his mouth until the whistle blew. He set his water bottle down and quickly skated to the circle. Down on one knee, he watched as Coach Green drew the next drill—a three-on-two. *Good*, thought Josh, who liked drills that were challenging and more like a real game.

The skills stuff was okay, but this was competition and way more fun.

When Coach Green announced the lines, Josh was playing centre between Peter on left and Graham on right. Kevin was on a different forward line, which was up first.

Josh watched as Kevin picked up the pass from the coach and headed down the ice. What a slick stick-handler! Kevin made one pass, then got it back on his stick and wove around the defence. Instead of passing he took a shot on net—right over Sam's shoulder into the top corner. Josh wished he could shoot like that.

Next was Josh's line. Heading into position, Josh wondered if Peter would pass. Often the most skilled players could score single-handedly by deking around everyone all the way down the ice. They might be stopped by a check, but no one was strong enough to check Peter.

The coach sent Josh a puck. Right away, Josh saw the defence in position, so he whacked it to Peter who was moving fast. At full speed, Peter picked up the puck and skated across the blue line. Peter's options were to take a shot, pass back to Josh, or send the puck over to Graham. Peter wound up for a shot. *So he's a hotshot just like Kevin*, thought Josh.

But Peter faked the shot and skillfully pulled the puck back, passing it through the defence and over to Graham, who was near the net. Josh saw his golden opportunity and rushed to the side of the net. Sam, who had been anticipating Peter's shot, suddenly realized that he had been outsmarted and swung over to cover the side of the net. But he wasn't quick enough. Graham nailed a wrist shot, and Josh deflected it into the corner of the goal.

"Great play," said Coach Green. He patted all three of them on the back when they returned to the lineup.

Even though Kevin had a helmet on, Josh could tell by the set of his shoulders that he was scowling.

9 STICKS AND STONES

By the time Josh had had his interview—he told the coaches he wanted to work on hitting, his slapshot, and skating—eaten dinner, and watched and analyzed a video, it was almost nine-thirty. He was out of energy. The rest of the gang were planning to play cards right until eleven o'clock lights-out. If he played cards that late it would be midnight before he got to sleep.

Finishing his nightly routine, including his snack before bed, Josh crawled into his sleeping bag at ten o'clock. Minutes later, Peter came into the room. Josh faked sleep but kept his eyes opened enough to watch Peter.

Peter's hair looked as if it had something in it, and he was walking in sock feet. Josh watched as he threw his shoes on the floor, snatched his towel from the back of a chair, and stormed out of the room—toward the showers, Josh presumed. What was in his hair?

Josh continued pretending to be asleep when Peter returned. Hunkered under his covers, Josh saw Peter fling his towel onto his desk. What was he so mad about?

Josh didn't move a muscle. He watched Peter strip to his boxers and sit on the end of his bed. When Peter rested his head in his hands, Josh wondered if he was crying.

But totally dry-eyed, Peter shook his head, crawled into his sleeping bag, and turned out his light. Josh closed his eyes. What had happened?

★★★

Tuesday morning at breakfast, Josh heard that some of the guys had decided playing cards wouldn't be as much fun as playing a few pranks. Peter had been their main target. They had thrown leftovers from dinner in his hair and put pudding in his shoes.

Kevin was laughing as he ate his scrambled eggs and toast. "Man, you should have seen his face when he put his feet in his shoes."

"Gross!" Rory stuck out his tongue.

"We'll have to think of something new to do," said Kevin. "It was hilarious to watch his face. Last year, at this other camp I went to, we had a blast playing jokes. Mike LeBlanc was the funniest."

"You went to camp with Mike LeBlanc?" Sam was impressed. "He's the best Bantam goalie in Canada. He's going to make the NHL for sure."

"He's a good guy," said Kevin. Then he did his cool hair flick. "But you guys are just as cool. Last night was so funny."

Josh glanced at Sam to see if he would say anything. He didn't want to be the only one who thought the pranks disgusting. But Sam had his head down and was shovelling food into his mouth.

On the way over to their morning ice session, Josh walked with Sam. "Did you help put pudding in Peter's shoes?" Josh asked quietly, so no one else could hear.

Sam shoved his hands in his pockets. "Not really. I watched."

"Peter was mad when he came in our room."

"They were just kidding around," said Sam. "I mean, it was food. Kevin was playing a little joke. He's just that kind of guy."

"Yeah," Josh said. "I guess."

The ice session, once again, was challenging. Josh loved how much the coaches helped with individual skills. Already, after just two days, he felt as if his shots were improving, and his hitting as well. They were teaching him anticipation and reaction, and how to work tough along the boards. Even with regular water breaks, though, Josh knew from the way his heart was pounding that his blood sugar was dropping. Had he given himself too much insulin again this morning?

In the dressing room after practice, he leaned back against the wall, closed his eyes, and listened to the dressing-room talk. He'd be okay—yesterday he'd survived without a snack till he got to his room.

"Hey, Eskimo boy, you like that pudding last night?"

he heard Kevin ask.

Josh didn't hear a reply.

"I'm talkin' to you, in the corna' of the room," Kevin rapped. All the guys laughed.

Josh opened his eyes and tilted his head forward to see Peter, who was almost dressed and totally ignoring Kevin.

Kevin wiped the ice off his skates and threw it at Peter.

Peter dodged the ice, stood up, and started to walk toward the door. Halfway across the room, Peter stopped in front of Kevin. "We are not Eskimos," he said through clenched teeth.

"You can talk." Kevin grinned.

"Shut up!" Peter stormed out of the dressing room.

When Peter had left, Kevin stood up on the bench. "Whoa," he said, raising his arms in theatrical gestures. "I didn't know guys living in that cold climate could be such hotheads. Get it?" Kevin laughed, jumping off the bench. "Doesn't he know I'm just joking?"

Josh quietly picked up the balled-up socks Peter had left behind. He noticed Sam wasn't laughing either.

All the players were to meet behind the arena at the tennis courts for today's dry-land, which was ball hockey. Walking outside in the bright sunshine, Josh glanced at his watch. He had thirty minutes to get his ball hockey stick from the room and eat. Excited about playing ball hockey, he needed food to play hard. This would be a good warm-up for the big game on the ice on Saturday, the last day of camp.

He walked slowly back to the dorm. Breathless, he entered the room to see Peter sitting on his bed, taping his stick.

"Ah, getting your stick ready?" Josh asked.

"You bet." Peter ripped the end of the tape and tossed the roll on his desk.

"I can't wait to actually play a game." Josh pulled out his snack box. After feeding all the guys, he knew his supply was rapidly dwindling. Josh threw Peter a granola bar. "For energy," he said. "Maybe we'll be on the same team."

"Maybe, maybe not." Peter attempted a smile. "Thanks," he said, giving Josh the thumbs up.

Josh gobbled down a few fruit leathers and some crackers. Then, after wiping the crumbs from his shirt, he said, "Come on. Let's go."

★★★

Josh ended up on the same team as Kevin and Sam. Sam was playing out instead of in goal. Peter was on the other team.

The pace of the game was fast. In ball hockey the bounce of the ball gave ample opportunity to score goals. Josh got two in the first half—one off a rebound from Kevin's shot, and another he flicked in the top corner after Sam made an awesome pass. Sam cheered and punched the air before he ran to Josh, giving him a high-five. Josh patted him on the back, happy to see his friend so excited with his assist. Kevin scored at least four for Josh's team.

For the other team, Peter must have scored eight. His hands were quick and he made most of his goals with a wrist shot to the top corner. Kevin and Peter weren't on together all that much in the first half, which was good, thought Josh. Ball hockey was fun, but playing without padding tempted injury.

Three-quarters of the way through the third period, the teams were tied. The sun beat down on the black pavement. Sweat poured off all the guys, but none of them cared—they all wanted the win.

Josh ran down the court and, seeing Sam on the far side, passed the ball over. Sam picked up the bouncing ball and took a shot on net. Rory, in net for the other team, made the save.

"Right at the goalie!" Sam exclaimed. "I should know better than that!"

"Next time," Josh said to Sam as they both ran to the sidelines.

Kevin was on next. Josh watched as he lined up in the end zone for the faceoff against Peter.

"This should be good," said Josh to Sam. He rested his chin on his stick. "I think Peter can beat Kevin." Josh wiped the sweat off his brow.

"I hope not," said Sam. "We want to beat these guys."

"You're right," nodded Josh, smiling at how pumped Sam was to be playing out. "Come on, Kevin, you can take this faceoff!" Josh yelled.

The ball dropped and both Kevin and Peter fought for possession. Kevin managed to send it back to Mike, who was on defence. Mike wound up for a slapshot, but faked it and passed back to Kevin. Kevin stickhandled the ball, looking for someone who was open. He saw his centre hanging close to the net and tried a quick pass. But Peter, coming from nowhere, intercepted! Running at full tilt, Peter had a breakaway. When he got close to the net, he fired the shot, ripping the ball to the back of the net.

"Man, he's good," said Sam.

The lines faced off at centre. This time, Kevin did some pushing and shoving to get the ball. Peter gave Kevin a push back and slapped the ball to one of his players. Kevin turned and cracked Peter with a rough cross-check. Peter stumbled but recovered to move in the direction of the play.

"Whoa," said Sam, glancing at Coach Green, who was on the sidelines with a whistle. "He must not have seen that."

"They're not calling any penalties," said Josh.

"Obviously not," replied Sam.

The goalie for Josh's team made a fabulous save and

Kevin's line ran over to the side.

"Go for it, guys," said Kevin. "Be tough. Roughing is not getting called."

Josh and Sam ran into position. Their shift went well and Sam managed to pop one in to tie the game. He jumped up and down in excitement.

Coach Green blew the whistle. "Last shift guys. It's almost time for showers and grub."

Again, Peter faced off against Kevin. They jostled for possession. The ball ended up bouncing toward a player on Peter's team. Peter took off, calling for the pass. When it did come his way, he ran full speed with the ball on his stick. Kevin also ran, back-checking like crazy. He managed to make up a few strides, but there was no way he was going to catch Peter before he shot on net. Kevin reached forward and stuck his stick under Peter's leg.

Peter went down face-first and skidded on the pavement.

Josh looked around to see if the coaches had seen the hook. But Coach Green lifted his head only in time to see Peter on the ground. He yelled from the other tennis court where he was busy picking up orange cones. "Hey, Peter, you okay?"

Peter waved him off. Josh winced when he saw Peter's injuries. Peter's knees were skinned and bleeding and full of little stones. Plus, his nose was scraped.

Kevin picked up the ball, ignoring Peter's fall, and

sent a pass up to one of his players, who deked around the defence and fired a shot into the net. Kevin jumped in the air, waving his arms in a victory dance. Sam also jumped up. Josh tried, but he didn't feel like cheering. What a dirty win.

Kevin came running over to slap hands. Then he turned toward the other team. "Hey, Peter, did you go for a *little sled*?"

Peter lunged at Kevin.

Kevin lost his balance for a few seconds, but then regained it to push Peter back. From Peter's scrunched-up facial expression it was obvious he wasn't going to ignore the taunts this time. He pushed Kevin hard. Then he balled his hands into fists. "I'll go a round with you," he said darkly.

"Hey, what's going on here?" Coach Green pulled Peter back by his T-shirt. Then he looked at Kevin. "I want to speak to both of you." Coach Green eyed the rest of the guys, who gathered to surround Peter and Kevin. "Everyone but Kevin and Peter, go for lunch."

10 DON'T GIVE UP

"What do you think will happen to them?" Sam whispered in Josh's ear as they waited for their cheese tortellini by the cafeteria counter. "Do you think they'll get kicked out?"

"Shhh." Josh leaned closer to Sam. "Kevin's here already. He's over by the salad bar."

Once their plates were heaped, Josh and Sam headed to an empty table. All the excitement had made Josh forget that he needed to fuel up. He was a bit shaky. As soon as he sat down, Josh started shovelling his food into his mouth. He had his head bent down to his plate when he heard Kevin.

"Hey, guys. How's grub today? I'm starving!" Kevin lifted his leg over the seat to sit at Josh and Sam's table. Rory and Nelson were right behind him, as were four other guys.

Josh moved down to accommodate everyone.

"Great win!" Kevin said jubilantly. He turned to Sam. "You're not bad for a goalie. You scored a few.

Good on ya."

Sam beamed. Josh remained silent, surprised at Kevin's chipper demeanor.

"What happened with the coaches?" Sam asked through a mouth full of food.

"Nothin'," Kevin said with an air of confidence. He ripped a piece of bread in half. "We won, didn't we? No one likes a sore loser." Kevin sopped his bread in his tomato sauce. "Eskimo boy had his chance to talk, but he didn't. That's not my problem. I love this meal."

"Maybe he doesn't want to be a big baby and that's why he didn't say anything. He was going to deck you," Rory said, raising his eyebrows.

"Never," said Kevin with attitude. "Even if the coaches hadn't come along, I would have pounded him back." Kevin chugged back a full glass of milk, wiped his mouth on his arm, then leaned forward. He eyed the table of guys. "Listen," he said in a hushed voice. "I've got some hilarious ideas. And you're all included."

★★★

Peter was lying on his back, staring at the ceiling, when Josh came in the room. His shins and nose looked like raw meat.

"Hey," said Josh, trying to be upbeat. "You eat already?"

"I'm not hungry," Peter said flatly.

"You gotta eat."

"I'll get something from the vending machine."

Josh opened the drawer of his night table and pulled out his snacks. "Here," he said softly. "Have some of this stuff. I have lots." Josh didn't have lots, not after Kevin and the other guys had raided his stash, but he couldn't let Peter go hungry.

"It's okay." Peter sat up. "I know you need that food."

Josh couldn't help but grimace when he looked at Peter's nose. "That looks so sore."

Peter sighed, blowing his air out in a loud sound.

Josh sat on the end of his bed. "I can't figure out why Kevin is so mean to you, except that you're as good as or better than him at hockey."

Peter looked straight at Josh. "You don't get it, do you?" Peter's voice was low and he had a weird puzzled look on his face. "Lots of people hate me." He paused. "When people think of hockey players they think of Joe Sakic or Mark Messier, not a guy like me. I'm a Native. Native people aren't supposed to be good at anything. Well, maybe hunting or drinking or whatever. Not hockey."

Josh didn't say anything. In a way, Peter was right. He didn't fit Josh's picture of a hockey player. But the picture was wrong...

"I wish I could hate hockey," mumbled Peter.

"Don't say that. You're good. You're, like, the best."

"It would make my life easier if I could hate it."

Peter stood. "I think I'll get something from the vending machine. You want anything?"

"Nah, I'm okay," said Josh. "I can't eat too much at one time. But after I do a few things here, I'll head back to the arena with you."

"I wish my mother had been as careful as you are," Peter said.

Josh shrugged.

"Just before she died I told her I would make her proud."

"I bet you can make the NHL if you keep trying. Or at least get a college scholarship or something."

Peter attempted a smile. "Thanks. You're okay, you know."

★★★

The afternoon ice session consisted of tons of breakout drills and power skating. Coach Green told them that if they worked hard they could have a ten-minute scrimmage at the end of practice. He wanted to get an idea of teams for Saturday's game.

Half-way through the practice, at his water break, Josh saw Kaleigh sitting in the stands. Before she left for summer holidays, Josh had given her the schedule and she had said she would try to attend a practice. She wore her blond hair in a ponytail pulled through a ball cap. Her board shorts and T-shirt set off her tan from her vacation in the interior of British Columbia. Pretending to concentrate, Josh didn't acknowledge her wave. He did hope, though, that he could talk to her after practice.

Kaleigh's presence in the rink gave Josh incentive. He hustled for every puck, digging in the corners, not afraid to take the hits.

Finally, Coach Green called them in and announced the scrimmage teams. Josh listened for his name. He was on a team with Peter and Sam! He skated over to the bench, noticing that Kevin was on the other team. Of course, it made sense that the two best players would be split and put on opposite sides. The coaches would be juggling the lines, trying to establish good combinations. They also wanted to make sure that everyone had a chance to play together. They said the camp was about building skill and part of that was learning how to be successful no matter who was on the line.

The game started off fairly even. At the five-minute mark, with the score tied 2–2, Josh stepped on the ice for his first shift with Peter.

"Peter, take centre," said Coach Hal. "Josh at right and Rory at left."

So far, Josh hadn't scored or got an assist. *And Kaleigh was in the stands.*

Josh lined up at centre ice. Peter looked over and gave him the nod. Josh bent over, anxiously waiting for the puck to drop. Peter fought for the faceoff. He won it but, because of the scramble, had to send it back to the defence instead of to Josh. Josh skated up his wing, hoping the defence would fire it his way. But the puck went to Rory on left wing. Peter and Josh rushed toward the end zone with Rory. Josh tried to get into a good position so Rory could make a pass, but he struggled in a tie-up. But Peter managed to get open—wide open!

Head up, Rory saw Peter but didn't pass. Instead he took the puck all the way down his wing and behind the back of the net, trying for a wraparound. No such luck. The goalie had the angle covered and snagged the puck with his glove.

Skating back to the bench, Josh asked Rory, "Why didn't you pass to Peter? He was in perfect position in the slot."

"I didn't see him," said Rory, not meeting Josh's eyes.

11 A TEAM-BUILDING TALK

Josh undressed quickly so he could get out of the dressing room and try to catch Kaleigh. He made up an excuse about having to go back to the room right away, and bolted up the stairs two at a time. As he ran into the lobby, he saw Kaleigh by the doorway with her father, ready to leave.

"Kaleigh," he yelled.

She turned and waved. "Josh. I didn't think you'd come up."

"We have an hour of downtime, before dinner," he said, puffing.

"That was a tough ice session, Josh," said Mr. Radcliffe. "You worked hard out there."

"They're all like that. But I'm learning a lot," said Josh.

"Good for you." Mr. Radcliffe touched Kaleigh's arm. "I'll bring the car to the front, okay?"

"Sure, Dad." Once her father had left, Kaleigh grinned at Josh. "Is it fun living in the dorms?"

"Ye-ah," said Josh, doing a Kevin-flick with his hair.

"Who's in your room?"

"You know the guy I was on the line with at the end?"

Kaleigh scrunched up her face. "You mean the guy who tried the wraparound when he should have passed?"

"No, the other guy."

Kaleigh raised her eyebrows and widened her eyes. "The really good guy. He is amazing. He can hit like the Juniors. And his slapshot is a bullet."

"Tell me about it. Sam says he gets blisters every time he saves one of his shots."

"Is he a fun roommate?" Kaleigh was totally interested.

"He's from up north. He even brought a drum with him."

"Really? Like a drum, drum?"

"Not a drum like a band drum," said Josh. "It's made from hide and wood. Remember that unit on the Inuit we did? That kind of drum."

"That is so cool!"

"I haven't heard him play it yet. We haven't had time." Josh glanced at his watch. "I got to go, Kaleigh."

"Hey, Josh," said Kevin from the other side of the lobby. "I thought you were getting a pop."

Josh winced when he heard Kevin's voice.

"Is that Kevin Jennings?" Kaleigh whispered to Josh.

Josh quickly nodded before turning to face Kevin, who was standing at the vending machine.

"Come on, Josh," whispered Kaleigh in Josh's ear. "Let's go see him. I want to meet him."

"Oh, all right," said Josh under his breath. Why did Kevin have to come upstairs today?

"Hey, Kev," said Josh, trying to be cool. "Watcha getting?"

Kevin punched the button for a red power drink. Pulling it from the slot, he said, "The good stuff." Then he smiled. "Is this Ka-leigh?"

"How do you know my name?" asked Kaleigh, puzzled.

"Josh talks about you all the time," said Kevin, grinning.

"I do not," exclaimed Josh.

"Yeah, right." Kevin rolled his eyes. He turned to Josh. "Hey, we don't have much time. I'll walk back with you."

Josh turned to Kaleigh. "I got to go."

"No prob," She said, but didn't move to go. When Kevin had turned toward the door she said, "Are you, like, doing okay with your diabetes?" Sometimes, she was overprotective, just like his mother.

"Yeah." He did feel really shaky from the practice but he said, "I'm doing great."

★★★

77

That evening there was video analysis. With the lights out and the room black, Josh fell asleep. When the lights came back on, he sat up in his seat, wiping his eyes. He felt faint and a bit nauseous, and he had pains running up and down his thighs. He knew his blood sugar was low and he had to eat something. Deep down, he realized he was doing what his doctor called "chasing his blood sugars." All his blood glucose readings had been inconsistent, so he just ate extra food or upped his insulin to help combat the reading, without ever being in control of stabilizing his blood sugar level.

"I'm going to bed," he said to Sam as they walked out.

"Bed? Already? It's only ten. We've got a card game to finish."

"I know." Josh wanted to play cards, but just not tonight. "Hey," he said. "Why don't we play tomorrow on the bus to Banff? Give us something to do for an hour."

"That's a great idea," said Sam. "I'll tell Kevin and maybe we can set up a tourney. I can't wait to go to Banff. We're doing that gondola up Sulphur Mountain."

Josh couldn't wait for tomorrow either. Although he hated to admit it, a day with just one ice session was going to be a good break.

Wednesday morning the sun shone in the sky like a brand new, yellow tennis ball. It was an absolutely perfect day for a trip to the mountains—not too cold or too hot. Sometimes, even in summer, Banff could be rainy and miserable and chilly. The difficulty on those days was actually seeing the mountains, and the wind could be cold at the top of Sulphur Mountain. But if the weather held, by afternoon the view would be clear and the air warm.

After breakfast and before their ice session, all players were supposed to meet in the Red Room for a team-building seminar. Then the schedule said the ice session was to consist of games like baseball and capture the flag—fun stuff. The coaches were going to set up an obstacle course. Josh liked the motivational talks way better than the nutrition stuff (he had his fair share of nutritional talks with his diabetes), and he loved playing games on the ice, especially scoring relays and races.

Coach Green had set up the screen projector at the front of the room. The room buzzed with energy, unlike the evening video analysis when everyone was trying to resist sleeping. After all the guys were seated and quiet, Coach Green introduced a special sports psychologist brought in specifically for this motivational talk.

Josh leaned over and whispered in Sam's ear, "This should be okay. He's worked with some teams in the Ontario Junior Hockey League."

Sam nodded. "I know. How cool is that?" he whispered back.

When the first overhead went up on the screen, Josh quickly wrote down the four quotes.

Respect: it's the cornerstone of a team player.
Take charge of your attitude. Don't let some-
one else choose it for you.
Park your ego at the door.
Pay the price for the person you sit next to.

"Okay, guys," said the psychologist. "All of these quotes may seem self-explanatory but let's go through each one individually."

He used a pointer to indicate the first quote. "Respect is important in all aspects of this game. Respect for yourself, your teammates, your opponents, and also your teachers, your parents, your siblings. You may think you just need to have respect for your coaches." He turned to look at Coach Green, who smiled and crossed his arms, then turned back to face the guys. "But respect is something you should practise with everyone you meet. People like store clerks, ticket takers at the movies. The harder you practise off the ice, the better you'll be on the ice and with your team. Respecting your fellow teammates is crucial to success, even if they are a bit different from you."

The psychologist paused then pointed to the second quote on the list. "I want to throw this one back to you. Give me some ideas as to what you think this one means—*Take charge of your own attitude.*"

Josh listened carefully and took notes, but didn't venture to put up his hand and answer. He wasn't good at answering questions in class—he got all clammy and his words always came out wrong.

Kevin put up his hand.

"Go ahead," said the psychologist.

"I think this means that as a player you need to show up to every game and every practice focused and ready to play your best. You can't be lazy for a practice because that kind of attitude will just make you lazy in a game."

"That's excellent. I especially like the point about showing up for every practice. Sometimes it's easy to say, 'It's just a practice—who cares?' Well, guys, elite players care. Let's move on. Any ideas about number three? *Park your ego at the door.*"

Mike raised his hand. "Don't think you're better than everyone else. And don't bring your attitude into the dressing room."

"That's right. Teams are teams. They're made up of individuals, each person with a different set of skills. Everyone has something to contribute and if you think that your skills are the only ones that are needed, then you're not helping your team."

After the psychologist read the last quote—*Pay the price for the person you sit next to*—he said, "Remember guys, it's important to work on the ice with everyone who sits on the bench. Not just a chosen few. Not just those who are your best friends, the ones you hang out with after the game or when practice is over. If someone you don't hang with is on your team and is making the shot, it doesn't matter who it is—you check the man in front of the net to give your teammate an opportunity to score. A team consists of every person who has been selected." The psychologist motioned for Coach Green to turn on the lights.

The lights made Josh blink for a few seconds. Then his attention was once more riveted to the front of the room. He had enjoyed this talk. The psychologist looked around the room. "You may think that this group you're with today isn't a team. I mean, you're just at a camp, right?"

No one answered.

"Most of you won't be teammates next season. You'll all go home to your communities and you'll play with players you already know." He crossed his arms and tilted his head as if he was thinking hard. Josh sat forward in his chair, waiting to hear his next words.

"If I were you guys," the psychologist paced the front, "I would use this opportunity, at this camp, to practise working as a team. And not just any team, a high-level team. Who knows, some of you may go on to play for a provincial or national team one day, and then you'll be expected to gel as a team in a camp situation just like this. Why not practise now?" He smiled. "Thanks, guys, for letting me join you today."

Everyone in the room cheered. Josh said to Sam, "I liked that. That was good."

Sam didn't answer because he was looking at Kevin, who was showing Rory and Nelson his paper. Written in bright red were the words *Take charge of your attitude*.

12 BUS TRIP TO BANFF

Josh dug his edges in and skated to the first tire. He landed his jump without a wobble. Next he skated to the hoop he had to dive through. Peter was racing against him on the other side, but he was just approaching the tire! The entire ice session had been fun games and this was the last race. Josh and Peter were the last two to go.

Josh dove through the hoop and immediately got up, trying not to slow down. Next, he had to skate around a cone, then he had to jump over another tire. Peter was catching up to him. Josh could hear his team shouting his name. He bent low and made a tight turn around the cone. As he finished his turn, he saw that Peter was just starting his. Josh lengthened his stride, hoping to clear the tire. He jumped—when he landed he felt the back of his skate hit the tire. He wavered before catching his balance.

Out of the corner of his eye, Josh noticed that Peter had cleared his tire too. They were now both skating full speed toward the finish. He kept up with Peter for half the ice, then Peter shot ahead, crossing the line two steps ahead of Josh.

Josh felt horrible. He'd let his team down. Kevin skated up to Josh and playfully punched his arm. "Don't worry about it. We'll get them next time. He's only good on a straightaway anyway."

Josh smiled, thankful for the words of encouragement.

★★★

Boarding the bus, Josh saw Peter sitting by himself near the back. Peter waved and Josh waved back. Josh started down the aisle to sit with Peter when he heard his name called. He turned to see Mike holding up a deck of cards.

"You're my partner," said Mike grinning. "We're playing Sam and Kevin in the first round. Kevin set up the tourney last night when you went to bed. We need to sit across from them." Mike paused for moment to study Josh's face. "Hey, you're not going bail on me, are you?" Mike was obviously desperate to play. For two days he'd been trying to get Kevin's attention and now he had a chance to play cards with him. "Come on," whispered Mike. "Be my partner."

Josh glanced down the bus at Peter and motioned that he was going to play cards. Peter nodded, held up his thumb, then turned his head to stare out the window.

By the end of the hour-long bus ride, the card game was over and Mike and Josh were victorious. Kevin was peeved.

"We lost on purpose," said Kevin. "I set up this tourney, you know, and Sammy-boy and I want to make the finals by sneaking in from the 'B' side. You see, we play the easy guys now then we'll meet you two again in the finals of this tourney. That is, if you're not knocked out first. So look out. We're not out yet."

"Geez, he takes his cards seriously," whispered Josh to Mike as he tossed his cards in the main pile.

"I heard that." Kevin leaned forward and looked at Josh. "You ever heard *Play hard…Play smart*? Or, *No regrets*? Or, *Never quit*? 'Cause I have. And I live by those quotes. In everything I do."

"Not everything." Sam grinned. "Not when you're snoring!"

"I don't snore." Kevin shook his head.

Sam laughed. "Oh yes, you do."

The bus lurched to a stop and Sam made a dumb fake dive. Josh laughed. They were at Sulphur Mountain already. He'd been so engrossed in the card game that the entire bus ride through the beautiful Rocky Mountains was a blur.

Suddenly, everyone in the bus started talking and the noise escalated. Josh couldn't wait to get off the bus and ride the gondola! He stood up and pushed his way into the line. All down the bus, guys were picking partners to ride with.

Kevin glanced to the back of the bus. Smirking, he turned back to Rory and Nelson. "Bets that Peter doesn't have anyone to ride with?"

"I'll ride with him," said Josh.

"Don't let him tell you anything about hockey," Kevin said with an exaggerated grimace, making everyone laugh. "They learn some strange things in his country."

"Duh. Where he lives is part of our country," said Sam.

"Yeah, well. He thinks he's better than us. He never talks to anyone. Come on, teammates. We're out of here. We need to ride together to discuss our plans. It's our job as team players to get him to be part of the team."

Walking down the bus aisle behind Sam, Josh whispered, "What plans is he talking about?"

Sam turned slightly and sheepishly raised his eyebrows. "I don't know."

"I don't believe you."

"Let it go, okay, Josh? It's nothing really."

When Josh stepped off the bus, his legs almost gave out on him. He pressed his fingers to his forehead, realizing that in the heat of the card game he'd forgotten to have a snack. Where was his backpack? He must have left it on the bus. Players were still unloading. He would have to wait to go back and get it. He tapped his foot, wanting everyone to hurry.

Finally, the last person was coming off the bus. It was Peter. He smiled and held up Josh's backpack. "This yours?"

"Thanks," said Josh, relieved.

"I figured you'd need it."

Josh took the backpack from Peter, unzipped the front pouch, and pulled out a fruit snack and a handful of crackers. He ripped open the wrapper and took a bite before he mumbled, "Sorry." His mouth was still full of food.

"For what?" Peter asked.

"Not sitting with you."

Peter stuck his hands in his pockets. "I don't care. I was too busy looking at the mountains. They're huge! Like massive chunks of rock."

"I kind of missed the view today." Josh crumpled his wrapper and shoved it in his bag. He slipped his pack onto his back. "You want to ride the gondola together?"

Peter tilted his head to stare up the mountain at the gondolas running up and down on cables. He was grinning when he looked back at Josh. "You're on."

Peter and Josh ended up riding the gondola with Coach Green and Coach Hal just to fill the cable car. Sam went with the other goalie and a few different guys. And Kevin, Nelson, Rory, and Mike all chummed together to get in the same car.

At the beginning, the ride was quite steep, and Josh saw Peter edge to the front of his seat.

"Whoa, this is cool," said Peter. "The land where I live is really flat."

"Wait till the top," said Josh. "You can see all of Banff." Although Josh had ridden this cable car a few times before, he still felt exhilarated. The view was spectacular. You could see the Bow River running through the town of Banff, Tunnel Mountain, the Banff Fine Arts Centre, the blue-green roof of the Banff Springs Hotel, and the golf course. And the higher they went, the more the cars far below looked like toys.

"Hey, look!" Peter exclaimed, pointing out the window. "A black bear!"

Josh leaned forward to get a better view and the car rocked a bit. Peter chuckled and moved back and forth to rock the car even more. Both boys laughed and continued rocking the gondola, even though it was a bit scary.

"Okay, that's enough, guys," said Coach Green, holding on to the hand grip. "Are you trying to make me sick?" He winked.

Peter smiled mischievously, rocked the car slightly, and bit his bottom lip to keep from laughing. Coach Green playfully shook his finger at him. "No more, wise guy."

Peter looked out the window again. "I can't see the bear now. You know, we have polar bears where I'm from. I've seen them when we're out hunting caribou."

"You hunt?" No one in Josh's family hunted. This was something new to him. Wasn't Peter too young to operate a gun? The thought of hunting always made Josh a bit squeamish.

"We have to eat," said Peter matter-of-factly. "If we don't hunt, we don't eat."

Josh could hardly believe Peter was talking so nonchalantly about killing animals.

"I've been up there, Josh," said Coach Green. "Hunting is a way of life. You use just about the entire caribou, don't you, Peter?"

"We eat the meat, and use the fur for coats and mitts and boots and stuff, if that's what you mean. And we use the bones for carvings. So, yeah, I guess we use the whole animal." He grinned impishly. "Not the brain though. Caribou aren't that smart."

"Eating the brain—gross!" exclaimed Josh. "Is hunting fun?" He'd never heard Peter talk this much. He hadn't realized his roommate was kind of funny.

"More like work," replied Peter, rolling his eyes. "Sometimes it's okay, but some days it's cold and really boring. You have to sit and wait. I hate the waiting part. I'd rather play hockey. But my dad, he doesn't let me play until my chores are done."

"We're almost there." Coach Green motioned outside to the person who was waiting to usher them out of their cable car before it went around the turn and back down the mountain.

The cable car slowed and the door opened. They had to move quickly because the car never stopped moving. If you didn't get out fast you'd end up riding the car to the bottom.

Josh quickly hopped out. He squinted into the bright sunshine. What a fabulous day to be on top of a mountain. Josh waved at Sam, who was up ahead on the walkway that led to the lookout station. He was horsing around with the other goalie.

Kevin also turned but he didn't wave. He just pressed his finger to his nose and mouthed, "Brown-noser."

13 PRETENDING

Sam sidled up beside Josh, who was standing by the railings at the very top of Sulphur Mountain. "Isn't this cool?" All the guys had hiked to the top lookout station. "I've only been up here once before and it was crappy outside. You couldn't see anything."

"I golfed with my dad this year at that Banff Springs course." Josh pointed toward the town of Banff and the big green space. "Hole number five is wicked."

"My favourite thing to do when I come to Banff is hit Welch's candy store," said Sam.

"I used to like that too."

"I'm sorry, Josh. I shouldn't have said that."

"No big deal." He shrugged. "Sometimes it sucks having diabetes. You didn't tell Kevin, did you?"

Sam shook his head. "Of course not." He paused. "But I don't know why you think it has to be a big secret."

"I don't want anyone to feel sorry for me or treat me like I'm different."

"I kind of feel sorry for Peter," said Sam quietly.

Josh stopped staring at the view of Banff to look at Sam. "Why is everyone so mean to him?"

"Some of the guys, well, they think he thinks he's better than everyone."

"He's just quiet," said Josh. "He's nice. And he's the best hockey player here but he doesn't act like he *thinks* he is." Josh's eyes scanned the group to find Peter.

Just as he spotted him in the crowd, Josh saw Kevin purposely walk into him so he fell forward. Peter stumbled and grabbed on to the railing. When he turned back, Kevin had run ahead, laughing.

"Do you like rooming with Kevin?" Josh asked.

"Josh, promise you won't tell anyone I told you this." Sam's voice warbled as if he was scared.

Suddenly, Coach Green yelled for everyone to find the group they rode up with. They were going to downtown Banff for a late lunch and for a trip to the candy store.

"I have to go find my guys," said Sam.

"What were you going to tell me?" Josh asked, grabbing hold of Sam's arm.

"Later, okay?" Sam pulled away.

Josh watched Sam run toward the other goalie. What was Sam's big secret?

★★★

Josh didn't get another chance to talk to Sam for the rest of the day. They were always surrounded by the other guys. After lunch they went to the candy store. Each boy had been told before camp started that they were going to have this adventure. Most parents had given money for the excursion.

"Hey, Josh," said Kevin standing behind him in line to pay. "Is that all you're getting?"

Josh, holding his one package of Skittles, said, "I'm not that hungry."

"No wonder you're so small and skinny." Kevin laughed. Then he picked up a large chocolate bar and thrust it into Josh's stomach. "Get one of these, they're the best. You eat the whole thing and it'll give you a wicked slapshot."

Sam, just ahead of Josh in line, turned and secretly handed Josh some money to pay for the chocolate bar. Josh's parents hadn't left him much money.

Outside the store, Kevin came up to Josh. "So, did you eat it yet?"

"No."

"What are you waiting for?"

Josh opened the candy bar and took a big bite. He remembered how he used to eat big chocolate bars like this before he found out he had diabetes.

While walking around downtown Banff, Josh ate the entire rest of the bar and a bunch of Sam's candy, plus his Skittles. He knew what he was doing was wrong—but what was one day? He'd be okay. He'd survived so far.

On the bus, Josh and Mike won their second card game—as did Kevin and Sam. One more win each and they'd be in the finals together. A lot of the guys were betting their candy on who would win, and the card tourney had become a big source of entertainment.

When they returned to the university, Josh wanted to walk with Sam and hear his secret but Sam had already taken off to his room. Josh needed to race back to his room and hit the washroom again, even though he'd gone a few times in Banff, and he was desperately thirsty. Closer to his room, he slowed down. He knew these were symptoms that his blood sugar was high. He grimaced. He'd eaten a whole bag of gummy bears on the bus after all the candy in Banff. If his mother found out, she'd never let him go anywhere by himself again. Who cared? His mother wasn't here. And he could do what he wanted. His doctor always said that slipping for one day wouldn't hurt.

As he approached his room, Josh could hear a weird noise coming from the other side of the door. Peter was playing his drum! Was he singing too? It didn't sound much like singing to Josh.

Josh slowly pushed open the door, not wanting to disturb Peter. For a few seconds he watched, with Peter not knowing he was there. Peter had the drum between his legs and was tapping it with his fingers almost as if he was playing the piano. Josh was awed by the speed of his fingers. Wouldn't that hurt? And the noise coming from Peter's throat sounded like warbling birds. How did he do that?

Josh tried to be quiet when he stepped in the room and shut the door, but he wasn't quiet enough. Peter stopped his strange singing and put his drum on the floor.

"Don't stop." Josh walked to his bed and sat down. He couldn't help but notice his blood monitoring kit, sitting on his night table. In his hurry this morning he must have forgotten to put it away. He didn't want to check his blood sugar.

"Play some more," Josh said to Peter.

"Nah, it's okay." Peter picked up his watch. "It's almost time for dinner anyway."

"How do you make those sounds?"

"It's throat singing. We do it lots where I live."

"Is it hard?"

"Not really. You have to use the vibrations in your throat to make the noises." Peter paused. "Like this." He opened his mouth and sang, sounding like a loon.

"Let me try." Josh tried, but he ended up making horrible squawking noises. Both boys laughed.

"Okay, so I suck. Let me try the drum."

Peter picked up the drum and handed it to Josh. "You have to hit it with the fleshy part of your finger. That gives you the best sound."

Again Josh tried, but the sound he made wasn't nearly as loud as what Peter could coax from the drum. "You get such an amazing sound," said Josh.

Peter turned his hands palm up. "Look at my calluses. I've been drumming since I was a baby."

"Does everyone drum up north?" Josh asked.

"Most do. But it's like hockey down here. Not everyone plays." Peter held up his watch. "It's almost time for dinner and I'm starving. I'll show you some more later on, if you want."

"Sure. Maybe tonight, after the movie. You know, you should really show everyone at the camp. I bet some of the other guys would think it was cool too." Josh picked up his blood sugar kit and opened the drawer to put it away.

"How many times a day do you check?"

Josh glanced up to see Peter staring at his blood monitor.

"I'm supposed to do four." Josh shrugged. "I don't feel like checking right now, though."

"Yeah, my mom hated doing it too. She pretended she didn't have diabetes. That's why she died."

Josh didn't know what to say. He felt uncomfortable when Peter talked about his mother. He reached in his drawer and brought his kit back out. He could die too, if he *pretended* he didn't have diabetes. He should check his blood sugar.

He poked his finger. He cringed when he looked

at his reading. It was high. Too high. He would have to give himself some insulin. While at the camp, he'd lowered his insulin doses because he was exercising so much.

Peter peered over at the reading on Josh's monitor. "My mom used to get higher readings than that. But that's still kind of high, isn't it?"

Josh scratched the back of his neck.

"Shouldn't you give yourself an injection?" Peter asked.

Josh pulled out his insulin pen. After adjusting the amount, he poked it into his abdomen.

"I wish she'd been careful like you," Peter said sadly. "Maybe she'd still be alive."

Without looking at Peter, Josh disposed of the needle in the sharps container. He didn't actually know of anyone who had died because they weren't careful with their diabetes. He'd read stuff the doctor had given him, but that was it. Josh's stomach did somersaults. Once in a while it was okay to go off track, at least that's what his doctor had told him, but then you had to make an effort to get back on track.

After dinner, Josh met up with Sam at the Red Room to watch an action flick.

"What were you going to tell me earlier?" Josh asked.

Sam hesitated and looked around the room. Finally he turned back to Josh and whispered, "You can't tell anyone I told you."

"Tell me." Josh leaned toward Sam.

"The guys are planning...they're planning to do some really awful things to Peter."

14 A MEETING

"What kinds of things?" Josh asked.

"They want to tie him up and force stuff down his throat! They've got it in their rooms. And they want to cut his hair weird and—"

"What do they want to put down his throat?"

"I dunno—gross concoctions. They've put shampoo in with pudding and apple sauce. Stuff like that. Nothing horrible that could hurt him. But that's not the worst of it."

"There's more?"

Sam grimaced when he nodded. "They want to rip his clothes off and make him walk back to his room naked."

"That's so unfair." Josh closed his eyes, thinking of how embarrassed Peter would be. It might even make him quit hockey.

"I know," said Sam. He hunched his shoulders. "I tried to tell them it's not right, but they said it's all harmless."

"Who's involved besides Kevin?"

"Rory, Nelson, and I think Mike might be now too. Plus, there are about four other guys. You know Kevin, he can get anyone to side with him."

"When were they planning to do these things?"

"Friday night. I think Kevin hopes Peter will be so mad that he'll play lousy on Saturday morning at the game. Between us, I think he's jealous of Peter."

"We should do something." Josh ran his hands through his hair.

"Yeah, but what?" Sam was exasperated. "What can we do? We can't fight Kevin. He's going to make the NHL!"

"Sam, we have to. Being the best has nothing to do with this. Remember what the psychologist said about respect. And what about *paying the price for the person you sit next to?*" Josh pressed his finger to his own breastbone. "I sit beside Peter on the bench sometimes. I can't let him down. This isn't fair. Just because he's from the North and plays a different style of hockey doesn't make this okay. They're all jealous."

"I know, you're right," said Sam blowing out air. He shoved his hands in his pockets. "But Kevin, you know, he might get all those guys against us."

Josh's temples throbbed, understanding Sam's worry. But what if Peter choked on all that gross stuff? He seemed to remember reading about something like this that had ended really badly.

"We need help," said Sam.

"Should we go to the coaches?" Josh asked.

Sam shook his head. "No, no. We can't look like rats. I have to room with Kevin." Sam paused. Then his eyes brightened a bit. "I got an idea. Why don't we phone Kaleigh? She's good at this kind of thing."

"Good thinking. You know, Kaleigh could help us research this, and then we could hold a meeting. Get everyone together and talk to them about how dangerous this is."

"A *meeting*? Are you crazy?" Sam looked horrified. "We could start a riot!"

Josh rubbed his hands together—they were sweaty and clammy. "I don't think we'll start a riot." He paused for a few seconds. "Do you really think that could happen? Stuff like that is only in the movies."

Sam's eyes were the size of saucers. "Let's phone Kaleigh," he said in a hurry. "She'll help for sure."

"When should we phone?"

"After the movie tonight," whispered Sam. "Let's meet by the phones in the lobby."

Josh fidgeted through the entire movie, unable to concentrate. Poor Peter. He'd be really upset if they did those things to him. But what if Sam was right and they did start some sort of riot? What if Kevin got everyone to jump Josh and Sam? Maybe they should just go to the coaches. But telling always made you look like such a big baby. No one did that sort of thing anymore.

A Meeting

Finally, the movie ended and Josh, trying to be as casual as possible, walked back to the dorms with Mike. He wanted to talk to Mike about the plans—but what if Mike told Kevin? Kevin might try to stop them from having the meeting. Instead, Josh talked to Mike about their next card game, which was to be against Sam and Kevin for the championship. They were playing the next afternoon.

Sam was waiting for Josh by the phone, which was tied up. Peter was talking to someone. When he saw Josh and Sam, he smiled and held up his finger to indicate he would be finished in a minute.

"Dad, I gotta go," said Peter. "Some guys are waiting to use the phone." He paused. "Yeah, see you Saturday." During the next pause he smiled. Then he said, "A hat trick! Okay, I'll try. Say hi to everyone else for me. And tell Susan congrats." He laughed before he quietly said, "I miss you too."

When he hung the phone up he said, "Sorry about that." He rolled his eyes. "My dad likes to talk about hockey. And my sister had her baby."

"Your sister had a baby?" Sam asked wide-eyed. "Wow, she must be way older than you."

"Fourteen. Almost fifteen, though." Peter shrugged. "Well, the phone is yours."

"Thanks," said Josh. At this point, knowing what he knew, he felt they just had to help Peter. None of this was his fault. Except for the fight with Kevin, he had basically minded his own business all week. And even then Kevin had pushed him into reacting. Josh didn't blame Peter for fighting back.

"See you in the room." Peter turned and walked down the hall.

Sam picked up the phone. "Come on. Hurry, Josh. There's no one in the lobby to hear us talking. Can you believe his sister had a baby? That's like Kaleigh having a baby in a year or so."

Kaleigh answered the phone after the third ring. To hear the conversation, Sam leaned toward the phone until his forehead was pressed against Josh's forehead.

"Josh, speak up," said Kaleigh.

"Sam and I need your help," whispered Josh.

In as few words as possible, Josh explained the situation to Kaleigh.

"That's so mean," she said when Josh had finished. "It almost sounds like hazing."

"Hazing?" Sam and Josh said the word at the same time.

"Shh." Sam looked around to see if anyone heard them. No one else was in the lobby yet. Sam sighed in relief.

"I read an article on it," said Kaleigh. "There was a school in the States where the guys who did the bad things got charged and went to court. Those guys at your camp could end up in jail!"

"Can you find that story on the Internet?" Josh

asked lowering his voice. "We need proof that this could get the guys in trouble."

"Sure. I'll do it now. Call me in the morning. Have you guys, uh, thought of going to the coaches?"

Josh curled his hand around the mouthpiece of the phone so no one could hear. "The guy who's planning it all is Kevin Jennings," he whispered.

"Kevin Jennings. Really? He seemed so cool."

"We don't want to look like wimps."

"Gotcha," said Kaleigh.

When Josh hung up the phone he turned to Sam and said, "I'm going to bed. I'm tired."

"How are we going to do this meeting thing?" Sam's eyes darted around the lobby.

"I don't know. Let's sleep on it and talk in the morning. Meet me here before breakfast tomorrow morning."

15 FACTS

Josh woke up Thursday morning feeling horrible. He had tossed and turned all night, twisting his sleeping bag around his body. At two o'clock in the morning he had had to get up to straighten his bag and go the bathroom. Now, the back of his head pounded and he felt nauseous. Of course, it didn't help that his mind had been racing all night with thoughts about the meeting. How were they going to do this?

After his morning routine—including eating the last snack in his box—he sped to the phone to meet up with Sam. Josh arrived first and waited by the phone, thinking of a plan. Suddenly, it came to him.

When Josh saw Sam fling open the door to the lobby, he ran toward him. "I've got an idea!"

Sam furrowed his brow while Josh explained how they could write notes saying the coaches wanted to have a special meeting and put them under the dorm room doors. They could have the meeting Friday morning. Everyone would come if they thought the coaches had planned it.

"But what if the coaches find out?" Sam asked.

"They won't. We'll wait until everyone is asleep to-night. Then we'll put the notices under their doors. If the meeting is first thing tomorrow morning, no one will have time to tell the coaches. If we meet at the arena all the guys will think they're announcing the teams for Saturday."

"Ye-ah. Okay," said Sam hesitantly. "Aren't you at all scared about doing this? What it if backfires?"

Josh rubbed his hands together. "I...I...it should work." He paused to blow some air out. His leg was shaking like crazy. He shifted onto the other leg. He finally cleared his throat and said, "For once, I want to make a stand about something." He clenched his fists. "What they're planning is wrong, Sam. Peter doesn't deserve this. We can't just sit back and watch."

"I know. I know," Sam sighed. "Let's make the notes after lunch."

Josh closed his eyes to think about the day ahead. They had to play...he opened his eyes and flatly said, "We can't. We have that card game. If we don't play they'll be mad at us."

"Ah, shoot. I forgot about that." Sam scrunched up his face.

Josh tapped his leg with his hand. "How about after video analysis tonight? It won't take long."

"Where are we going to get paper?"

"I've got some in my diabetes log book."

Sam attempted a smile and fake punched Josh on the arm. "Hey, your diabetes has come in handy. See, it's not so bad after all."

"Come on, let's phone Kaleigh."

"Listen, Josh." Kaleigh spoke fast. "An incident happened at a school in the States, with a football team. They were attending a football camp and the guys did horrible—and I mean horrible—things to some of the younger players. One guy went home and told and three guys got *prosecuted*."

"Kaleigh's talking in big words," mouthed Josh to Sam.

Kaleigh continued talking. "One of the guys almost died, Josh. You have to help. What if this Peter guy ends up in the hospital?"

Josh hung up the phone, more nervous than ever. Peter's life was in danger.

★★★

Remembering what Peter had said about his mother, Josh made sure he ate right at breakfast. The extra attention to his diabetes showed on the ice—he was focused. Even the coaches noticed. Coach Green came up to him during a hitting drill and commented on how well he was playing.

At dry-land Josh found himself paired with Peter

for the balancing exercises. Josh was dripping with sweat when the session was over, and wanted to get back to take a quick shower before lunch. He wouldn't have any time after lunch—the card game was on. Most of the guys were betting on Kevin and Sam. A few had said they would put their odds on Mike and Josh.

After lunch, Josh had to make a quick pit stop at his room. Peter was lying on the bed, reading.

"Good luck today."

"Are you talking about the card game?" Josh was surprised Peter was interested.

"Kevin always scratches his thigh when he's cheating." Peter sat up.

Stunned, Josh stared at him.

"It's true. I've watched him. He looks at his hand, knows he doesn't have the cards, says that he does and scratches. It's a real small move—he scratches with his index finger—but he does it every time. I wanted to bet a bag of Skittles on you guys but the jerk said I couldn't."

"Why?" Josh asked.

Peter shrugged. "Kevin said betting was closed. I can't stand that guy."

"Have you ever thought of beating the crap out of him?"

Peter nodded. "Oh, yeah—big time. But when Coach Green came to my hamlet he gave me some different quotes from the ones that other guy gave us. The one I always think of when Kevin's bugging me is *Emotional control: just walk away*! Coach Green uses it to get guys to stop fighting on the ice, but I use it off the ice for guys like Kevin." Peter smiled vindictively. "Watch for his little sign and you'll nail his butt to the wall."

★★★

Josh and Mike beat Sam and Kevin in record-breaking time. Josh could hardly contain his smirk whenever Kevin scratched his leg. Kevin tried to cheat and not get caught, but Peter was right—Kevin was cheating every time he scratched his leg—and Josh nailed him on it every time. A few times Josh had to look down so no one would notice him grinning. And once when he looked away, he saw Peter off in the distance giving him the thumbs-up.

When the game was over, Kevin threw his cards in the pile. "How'd you win?"

"I took your advice. *Play hard and play smart*." Josh could not help but smile. "Or how about…" Josh picked up the unruly stack of cards and neatly put them in a pile before he handed them over to Kevin. "…*No regrets*."

It seemed a lot of the guys had a bit more respect for Josh after the card game. That could go a long way at the meeting. Josh needed all the confidence he could get.

The rest of Thursday cruised by with another ice session, dinner, then a video analysis. Josh wanted the day to keep going because he knew that when it ended he had to get together with Sam and write the notes. Josh's stomach did backflips thinking about standing in front of the guys and challenging Kevin.

Josh went through his nightly routine as if everything was normal. He even went so far as to crawl into his sleeping bag. His plan was to meet Sam in the hallway once both roommates had fallen asleep. Josh had hidden his flashlight, paper, and two pens under his pillow.

Finally, he thought he heard Peter snoring. In the dark, he slipped out of his sleeping bag, grabbed everything he needed, and tiptoed to the door.

In the hallway, he saw Sam. He too had brought his flashlight.

"This is freaky," whispered Sam. "I hope we don't get caught."

16 THE NOTE

"What was that?" Sam looked around. No lights were on except the little red *Exit* sign.

Josh held his breath and listened. Working in the dark was eerie. "Nothing," he whispered to Sam. "It was probably just the wind. Keep writing. We're almost done. Did you bring the list of rooms?"

Sam nodded. "We'll have to shine our lights on the door numbers though. Or we'll never see them."

Josh wrote, *Special Meeting* in big letters. Then he wrote *Hockey Canada Lobby at 7:30 a.m.* That would give them a half hour before breakfast. Josh and Sam had decided that, for the why, they would write, *Big Surprise*.

"I'm sure these will work." At the bottom of the note Josh wrote, *The Coaches*.

"Everyone will come if they think the coaches planned this meeting," whispered Josh.

"This is my last one," said Sam. "Are you done?"

Josh gathered all the supplies and stood. "What's the first room number?"

Within fifteen minutes Josh and Sam had put the notices under every door. "I'll have to be real quiet going into my room," said Sam, his voice quivering.

"If Kevin wakes up, just tell him you had to go to the bathroom. And don't forget to put a note in your own room."

"I won't," said Sam. "See you in the morning."

As Josh crept back to his room, his stomach felt sick. Why had he decided to do this? How was he going to stand in front of the guys and talk?

Strangely enough, Josh fell asleep as soon as he curled into his sleeping bag, and he didn't wake until Friday morning. When he did open his eyes he jumped out of bed and glanced at his clock, realizing he had only five minutes before he was to meet Sam.

Josh quickly dressed and shut off Peter's alarm clock so he would sleep in—he couldn't find out about the meeting. With his snack box empty, Josh would have to go to the arena without eating anything. The night before, he planned to get something from the vending machine, but now he didn't have time. No big deal; he felt fine. Josh guessed what his blood sugar would be, hurriedly prepared his dose and jabbed the needle in his abdomen.

Sam was waiting for Josh outside. They walked briskly toward the arena.

Sam nervously licked his lips. "Kevin was up before I left. I told him I was going to the bathroom to get out of the room."

"What did he say about the note?"

"He thinks they're telling us our teams for tomor-row—you know, Saturday's big game. He hopes they're giving out sweaters. You know, white versus red. He did think it was weird that the note was handwritten, but I said I saw Coach Green last night and he was complaining about the photocopier being broken."

"Smart thinking."

"I don't feel so good about this."

"We have to put a stop to what they're planning," Josh replied, desperately hoping he sounded confident.

"I know, but couldn't we have figured out another way?"

"It's too late now." Josh picked up his pace until he was almost running. "Come on, we have to be the first ones there."

When Josh entered the Hockey Canada Lobby, he looked for something to stand on. He found a chair over by the wall. "This should do," he mumbled to Sam.

Sam nodded his head.

Within a few minutes, the guys started to file into the lobby. They were all discussing the reasons they thought the coaches would call a meeting first thing in the morning.

"Why didn't they have us come early to the first ice session?" Kevin asked, rubbing sleep out of the corner of his eyes.

"Or make an announcement at breakfast?" Nelson piped up.

"Where are they?" Mike looked around the lobby. Then he glanced at his watch. "They're late."

Sam nudged Josh in the ribs. "I think everyone's here," he whispered.

Josh rubbed the back of his neck and took a deep breath. What if he opened his mouth and no words came out? What if his voice squeaked?

The noise in the room seemed to be getting louder. All the guys were talking about why the coaches hadn't arrived yet.

"Come on, Josh," whispered Sam. "You've got to start."

Josh stepped up on the bench. From his position he could see the top of everyone's head. "Can I...can I have everyone's attention?" He heard himself yell.

All the guys turned to stare at him. His legs felt like pudding. He looked for Sam. Sam mouthed the word, "Talk!"

"Um," he started. "Sam and I have called this meeting to—"

"What!?" yelled someone. "I got out of bed early for you guys?!"

Josh held up his hands. This was not going how it was supposed to. "Just listen," he said loudly.

"Why should we listen to you?" a guy from the crowd interrupted.

"Yeah," someone else chirped.

Josh searched the room for Sam. Where was he? Josh saw him standing way by the corner. He was shaking his head, his eyes wide with fear.

"We have something to talk about that's important." Josh spoke as loud as he could without screaming.

"What's more important than breakfast?" This comment made some of the guys burst out laughing.

"Respecting our fellow teammates!" Josh raised his hands in the air. "That's what's more important. All those pranks you want to—"

"I'm hungry!" This time the voice was Kevin's.

"Me too."

"Me three."

Rory body-slammed Nelson. Laughing, Nelson fell to the floor.

"Hey!" Kevin hip-checked Rory, sending him flying. Suddenly all the guys were laughing and cheering and the meeting was totally out of control.

Josh couldn't believe how badly it was turning out. No one was listening. No one was going to hear what he wanted to say. The faces in front of Josh started to get blurry. He tried to focus.

Suddenly, Josh saw the coaches walking through the doors. Oh no! What a disaster!

17 COACH'S INSTRUCTIONS

"What's going on?" Coach Green asked, pulling the guys off each other.

"None of us really know," said Kevin, brushing dust off his pants.

Coach Green held up one of the notice sheets.

"Someone must have dropped this in the hall," he said accusingly. "I'd like to know what's going on here. Anyone care to tell me?"

Josh was trembling. "Um, this is…all…my doing."

"And m-mine too," said Sam, his voice quaking.

"Explain, please." Coach Green raised his eyebrows and spoke in that serious, adult, you're-in-trouble voice.

Josh's legs were shaking so hard his knees were knocking together. How did he get himself into such big trouble? He hardly ever got into trouble. "We just wanted to talk to the guys and, uh, we thought that if we said the meeting was with the coaches everyone would come."

Coach Green puckered his lips and tilted his head.

"And what was your purpose?"

Josh scuffed his toe on the floor. What should he say? "We wanted to talk about respect for other players." He knew he was talking too fast but he couldn't stop himself. "And about how players shouldn't be treated poorly because they have different backgrounds. We wanted to tell the guys that tying someone up or making them walk naked and doing other mean things could maybe make them go to jail. There have been kids from other teams who have done things and there have been serious injuries. And kids got charged. We have stats." Josh stopped talking for a minute to take a breath. His words had been like one big sentence.

Coach Green squinted and looked around the room. "Where's Peter?"

No one said anything.

Coach Green did a quick head count. "How come he's the only guy missing?"

"I heard rumours," said Graham quickly, "but I wasn't involved."

"What kind of rumours?" Coach Green asked firmly. "Someone, please, I want the truth."

No one said anything.

"We won't go on the ice until this is resolved," said Coach Green.

Mike lowered his head. "Some of us guys were going to play some pranks on Peter," he uttered.

"I wasn't involved," Graham said again.

"Me neither," said another guy.

Everyone started talking.

"Okay, guys." Coach Green sighed and held up his hands to quiet the room. "I'm very disappointed in your behaviour." He shook his head, obviously saddened by the situation. "I want everyone inside the arena, sitting in the bleachers just below the canteen."

All the guys filed into the arena. No one said a word. Josh kept his head down—he didn't want to see if anyone was glaring at him. Sticky sweat beaded on his forehead, his stomach flip-flopped in nervousness, and his heart was pounding. He felt really shaky—he hadn't eaten yet.

In the arena, Sam and Josh sat together. Coach Green stood in front of everyone with his arms crossed. "I expected more from this group," he said. "This *elite* group. Now, I want answers." Coach Green held up the sign he had found on the floor. "Josh, Sam—you start."

"Um," said Josh. He was having a hard time concentrating. "We, uh, made signs for a meeting because we didn't think that the pranks were okay. We, uh, thought someone might get hurt."

Coach Green still had his arms crossed. "Why wouldn't you come to the coaches with this?"

"I don't know." Josh shrugged, looking at Sam.

"You realize this meeting could have been a catastrophe?"

"I do now," said Josh.

"Your intentions were right but your method was wrong. I think it would have been a smarter move if you had come to us and let us handle this situation, instead of lying about a meeting."

"Sorry," mumbled Josh.

"Me too," said Sam.

"Now, for the rest of you guys." Coach Green paused to look around. The silence was horrible. "I want to know about these pranks. Mike, I'm not picking on you or saying you're the only one involved, but since you volunteered to talk a few minutes ago, maybe you could go first."

Mike eyed the guys. "Well, uh, some of the stuff was just stupid, silly stuff. Like, we put pudding in his shoes and crap in his hair."

"So, you've already done some of this stuff? Rory, do you have anything to add?" Coach Green looked directly at Rory.

"Not really. It was all just for fun."

"Fun? Kevin, how about you explain what fun was going to happen next?"

"Well, we, uh, made up kind of like a drink with stuff in it and we…"

"Finish, please."

Kevin traced squiggly lines on his pants. "We… were going to make him drink it."

"Make him drink it? How?"

Kevin stalled.

"I'm waiting for an answer, Kevin."

"We were…going to put him in a chair." Kevin lowered his head.

"*Put* him in a chair?" Coach Green shook his head in disgust as he looked around the group. "You mean, *force* him to sit in a chair. How, boys? Were you going to physically hold him down? Or maybe tie him up? This doesn't sound like silly stuff to me. This is not how human beings should behave to other human beings. Nor is this how teammates should behave toward other teammates. Plus, this is considered assault and a *crime*. Do you understand what I'm saying?"

Everyone hung their heads.

"Do you realize that you could have injured this person? Fellas, this is called hazing. There are documented cases where *silly pranks* have gone very wrong. And guess what—the consequences are huge." Coach Green paused. Then he said, "Kevin."

Kevin looked up.

"I expected more from you," said Coach Green. "You're a leader in this group and you've abused that. Weren't you a captain last year? Is this how you think a captain should act?"

Kevin lowered his head in shame.

Coach Green returned his attention to the group. "If I hear one word about anyone blaming another player for any of this, I will—and I mean it—send that person home. Let this all be a learning experience for everyone. Now, go for breakfast and make sure you show up for the ice session prepared and ready to work as a team."

The noise of the door being flung open at the top of the landing made everyone turn.

"Peter," said Coach Green.

Peter stood on the top platform holding a piece of paper. He held up the note Josh and Sam had made. "I found this in the hall. I heard voices in here from the lobby. I'm sorry I'm late."

When Josh looked up at Peter his vision blurred. His body felt floppy and he knew his blood sugar was dangerously low. Time had slipped by and he should have had breakfast by now. He blinked to try to get rid of the blurriness. His body wavered—he put his hand down on the bleacher for stability and took deep breaths.

"Josh, are you okay?" Sam whispered. "You're kind of white."

"I need sugar," said Josh.

"Coach Green!" Sam stood up. "Josh needs sugar!"

"I've got change. I'll get a pop!" Peter yelled from the top of the bleachers.

"What's wrong with him?" Kevin asked. All the guys circled Josh.

"Here, Josh," said Peter, panting from running to get the pop. "Take a sip of this."

Shaking, Josh grabbed the pop and downed half of

it in one swig. He closed his eyes to let the sugar take effect. He had been stupid in all kinds of ways this morning.

"Guys, back up a bit. Give him some space." Coach Green motioned for everyone to move back.

"What's wrong with him?" Kevin asked again, after moving.

"He has diabetes and his body needs sugar," said Coach Green. "How are you feeling now, Josh?"

"Much better."

"You have diabetes?" Kevin asked in astonishment, looking at Josh. "Wow. You never told anyone. My Grandpa had it. And so does the Philadelphia Flyer GM Bob Clarke. He's still my dad's favourite player."

"Bobby Clarke." Coach Green shook his head. "My first year in the NHL, I played against him. He was *tough*. And man, could he ever put the puck in the net." Coach Green eyed Kevin. "I bet your dad remembers Reggie Leach too."

"Reggie Leach?" Kevin shrugged. "Did he play with Bobby Clarke on that Philly team?"

"Reggie was an aboriginal hockey player from Flin Flon, Manitoba. He was Bobby Clarke's best friend. I think you should ask your dad about him." Coach Green turned and smiled at Josh. "Do you feel strong enough to walk?"

"Yeah. I really need some breakfast," said Josh.

★★★

In the cafeteria, Josh sat with Peter and Sam. Kevin sat at another table with some of the other guys. Josh noticed that Kevin kept looking over at them.

"Thanks for getting me the pop," said Josh to Peter.

"You were quick," said Sam. "Like real quick. You knew exactly what to do."

"My mom had diabetes too," said Peter quietly.

"I wonder when we find out about our teams for tomorrow." Josh didn't want to talk about diabetes anymore.

"Coach Green said today. I hope I'm not with Kevin," said Peter. "He never passes the puck to me." He stood up. "I have to go now. Coach Green wants to meet with me. I don't know what for."

Josh met Sam's eyes over the rim of his glass. They knew Kevin and some of the other guys had been asked to go to the arena early too, to talk to Coach Green.

18 GAME DAY

The next day, Josh awoke excited. He got up and shook Peter. "Hey, wake up."

Peter tossed his sleeping bag off the bed. "Game day!"

Last night the team list had been posted. Josh was on the same team as Sam, Peter, and…Kevin. Just before bed, however, Peter and Josh had made a pact that they wouldn't let Kevin ruin their final day at camp. No matter how hard he tried.

Josh leaped up. "We're supposed to pack first," he said as he landed. He opened up his suitcase and chucked all his clothes in without folding any of them. "My mom will do laundry when I get home."

"My dad too," said Peter, grabbing his old canvas bag. "He's coming to the game."

"My folks will be here too," said Josh. "And my sister and brother and maybe Kaleigh."

"Whoa, Kaleigh," ribbed Peter.

"Oh, be quiet."

Peter stuffed his bag with his clothes. When he was finished he stood and looked at Josh. "Thanks," he said embarrassed.

"For what?" Josh asked. Josh and Peter hadn't talked about what had happened. Josh didn't have the guts to ask how the meeting went. Anyway, when they found out they were on the same team, all they talked about was hockey and making plays.

"You shouldn't have gotten yourself in trouble for me," Peter replied. "Kevin and some of the other guys had to say they were sorry, although I still don't think Kevin likes me very much."

"Yeah, but if you hadn't run so fast to get me a pop, I might not have played today. We're even." Josh opened the drawer of his night table and pulled out his diabetes kit.

"Let's talk on the Internet when we get home," said Peter.

Josh pulled out some paper. "Good idea, write down your address."

After writing down their e-mail addresses, Josh tested his blood sugar. "Do you really think you'll move and billet with a family to play hockey?"

"I don't know," said Peter, picking up the picture of the young woman with the baby.

"Would you miss your family?" Josh pulled out his insulin pen and dialed up the correct dosage.

"Ye-ah. But it might be the only way for me to play

hockey. Did I tell you my sister just had a baby?"

"Is that her in the picture?"

"No, this is my mom…and me. When I was a baby. I know I would miss my family if I billeted, but I love hockey. And I want to play in the NHL. I told my mom I'd do it for her."

"Then you will have to move to make the big leagues. I hope I make the NHL too."

"Wouldn't that be cool if we ended up on the same team?"

"Cool? That would be awesome!"

"Come on, let's hurry," said Peter. "I'm starving and need breakfast."

After breakfast, Josh and Peter ran back to their dorm room. They were supposed to leave their bags in the Red Room before the game. The dorms had to be cleared by ten.

Josh was zipping up his bag when he heard a sound at the door.

"Knock, knock." Josh's dad stood at the doorframe. "Can I come in?"

Josh jumped up. "Dad! You're here early."

"I couldn't keep your mother away any longer. She's waiting in the Red Room. I thought I'd help with your bag." He smiled. "So, how was it?

Josh grinned. "It was awesome! I learned so much, Dad—you should see my slapshot now."

Peter grinned and Josh threw a pillow at him. "Okay,

so it's still not great. You should see *his* slapshot." Josh gestured to Peter. "It's almost as hard as Matt's."

"I'm looking forward to watching you boys play."

"I wonder if my dad's here," said Peter as he threw his duffle bag over his shoulder.

"Let's go see," said Josh.

Entering the Red Room, Josh immediately spotted his mom and Amy. Amy came running over, almost knocking Josh down with a big hug.

"Whoa, Amy," Josh laughed.

"Josh, honey." His mom also hugged him. "I missed you."

"Yeah," said Amy. "The house was too quiet. And every meal, Mom wondered if you were okay. It got so boring."

As Josh pulled back from his mother, he noticed Peter looking around the room.

He was just about to introduce Peter to his parents when Peter's face lit up.

"There's my dad!" Peter waved at him.

Peter's father, who was drinking coffee from a cardboard cup, waved back and walked toward them.

"Hey, Pete, did you have a good time?" He patted Peter's shoulder.

"The coaches were really good, Dad." He playfully shouldered Josh. "This is my roommate."

Josh's father stepped forward and held out his hand. "I'm Steve, Josh's dad. And this is my wife, Ellen. It looks like the boys survived."

Peter's father returned the handshakes. "Jim Kuiksak. Pleased to meet you both." He raised his eyebrows. "This was Pete's first time away from home."

"Josh's too."

"Hey," said Josh to Peter. "You should come and visit us this winter. That would be awesome."

"Can I, Dad?" Peter beamed.

Peter's father laughed and tousled Peter's hair. "Let's talk later. Shouldn't you guys be heading to the arena to get dressed?"

The boys looked at each other, handed their bags to their fathers, and ran out of the room, taking the stairs two at a time.

★★★

When he stepped on the ice, Josh noticed his family and Kaleigh and her dad in the stands. He wanted to show them how much he had improved. And he wanted to show his mother that he could take care of his diabetes all by himself. As much as he didn't want to admit it, he'd missed them all a lot.

The whistle blew for the first faceoff.

Josh was on right wing, Peter was at centre, and Mike was on left wing.

Peter managed to tip the puck back to the defence. Mike rushed up his wing, as did Josh. The defence threw the puck up the ice and Mike picked it up along the boards. He batted it off the boards and tried to skate around, but it was picked up by Graham on the other team.

Josh skated, back-checking. Graham took the puck around the net. Then he made a pass to his winger, Nelson. Josh saw his opportunity and rushed to the boards. He squared his body and checked Nelson against the boards. He was surprised to realize that his hit had been hard enough to make Nelson lose possession.

Josh's defence hustled to the puck and passed it to Peter, who was moving forward. Peter took off with the puck. Josh shook the kinks out of his body from the hit and skated up the ice. Peter passed to Mike.

Mike skated a few strides, making a few dekes, and Josh thought he was going to try to shoot on the net. Josh followed behind for the rebound.

But then Mike, instead of shooting, made a drop pass to Peter. Peter one-timed the puck, but shot right at the goalie, who caught it no problem. Josh rushed to the net for the rebound but the goalie wasn't giving it up. Josh skated over and patted Peter on the back.

"We'll get it next time," said Josh.

"Good hit," replied Peter. Then he turned to Mike. "Nice pass."

Mike nodded and skated to the bench.

Kevin's line was out next. He managed to win the faceoff and make a clean pass to Rory, who tried to skate up the boards. Before he could pop it off the boards, he was stopped by Brady with a good clean check. The puck became loose. Brady went after it, as did Kevin. They battled and Kevin ended up with the puck on his stick.

"Go wide, Rory," yelled Coach Green from the bench. "Give him someone to pass to."

Rory skated wide and Kevin threw him a pass. Rory picked it up, but then he overskated the puck and it got tangled in his feet. He tried to kick it forward, but Brady scooped it on his stick and sent it up the boards and out over the blue line. They skated down the ice. The play circled around Sam, and Brady managed to get a wrist shot off. Sam easily made the glove save and threw the puck out to his defence. Heading back up the ice, Rory bashed the bench with his stick. He wanted off—but Mike, his winger, was fixing his equipment.

"Peter, go out for Mike." Coach Green shoved Peter out the gate. Peter and Kevin were out together!

Josh saw his winger approach the bench so he stepped on the ice too, racing with Peter toward the net. Kevin was behind the net with the puck, stick-handling, looking for an open player. By now, Peter was out front, circling, trying to stay open. The defence was tough, pushing him around. Josh skated along the boards and called to Kevin.

Kevin looked up and made the pass. Josh saw Gra-ham —the other team had made a line change too—

coming toward him. Should he try his quick turn move? It had worked on Kevin in practice. He had to do something—Graham was going to crunch him. Kevin was still behind the net. Peter was still in front. Josh ducked and fired the puck to Kevin. Graham crashed into the boards as Josh fell to his knees.

Kevin picked up the puck and tapped it to Peter. Peter one-timed it. The goalie made an unbelievable block. Josh rushed to the net. The puck was loose! Kevin went for the rebound…and backhanded it into the top corner. What a shot!

Josh didn't pat Kevin's back but he did say, "Awesome goal, Kevin."

"Yeah, good goal," said Peter, nodding his head.

Kevin adjusted his helmet before he turned to Peter and said, "I can't believe he stopped your shot." Then Kevin skated to the bench.

Josh and Peter skated to centre ice. Kevin was now off and Mike was on. Peter was lined up for the faceoff.

As Josh got in his crouch, waiting for the puck to drop, he realized that although he may not have scored a goal this shift or even got an assist, he had done something else. Things were still not perfect, but Josh had stopped an incident that could have been dangerous and hurtful. He had stopped the roughing. He had stood up for what he believed in. He had scored. Big time.

ACKNOWLEDGEMENTS

Thanks to the editorial team at Lorimer, whose comments and insight made this a better book. Thank you Allison Husband from the Diabetes Clinic D.A.T. Centre at the Alberta Children's Hospital for ensuring the medical facts in this story are correct. Sean and Maria, thanks again for answering my questions—and keep playing hockey, Sean. An enormous thank you goes to Larry Lund from the Okanagan Hockey School for providing hockey school information, promoting *Interference*, and for being such a positive person. And, of course, no book is a book without readers, so thanks to you the reader.

MORE SPORTS, MORE ACTION
www.lorimer.ca

CHECK OUT THESE OTHER HOCKEY STORIES FROM LORIMER'S SPORTS STORIES SERIES:

Danger Zone
By Michele Martin Bossley

Jason Briggs is the star defenceman on his hockey team, and the toughest checker in the league. But when Jason accidentally checks a player from behind, the boy is seriously hurt. Now the boy's parents want him suspended for good. But how will Jason survive without hockey? Somehow, he must find a way to clear his name—but the odds seem stacked against him.

Deflection!
By Bill Swan

Jake and his two best friends are members of the same league team, the Bear Claws. They may not be "the worst team ever," but there sure is room for improvement—and when they face the Cougars in the city championship, they want to be on top of their game. But personal rivalries and interference from Jake's three all-too-supportive grandfathers start to create tension among the players. Can the Bear Claws get their rhythm back before the big game?

Delaying the Game
By Lorna Schultz Nicholson

All-girls hockey is a whole different world for Kaleigh—there are new teammates, new rules, and new problems to deal with. And when Shane comes along, Kaleigh finds that the world of boys has become just as confusing. Can she stick to her goals and rediscover her love for hockey, or will these distractions throw her off her game for good?

A Goal in Sight
By Jacqueline Guest

Aiden is the toughest defenceman in his Calgary hockey league, often spending as much time in the penalty box as on the ice—and that's the way he likes it. But when he hits another player after a game, Aiden finds himself charged with assault and sentenced to one hundred hours of community service. Unfortunately, Eric, the blind hockey player he's assigned to help, is not exactly what he had in mind...

Hat Trick
By Jacqueline Guest

Leigh is one of the top players on her hockey team, the Falcons—but she's also the only girl and a Métis, and not everyone is happy about that. Soon Leigh's receiving threatening messages, the Falcons' captain tries to get her kicked off the team, and to make matters worse, her mother wants her to perform in a dance recital on the same night as the championship game. When the pressure becomes too intense, Leigh has to face some tough decisions.

Hockey Night in Transcona
By John Danakas

After years of playing shinny, Cody Powell's dream has come true—he has made it onto the Transcona Sharks, the local league team, and it's finally his time to show everyone what he can do. But when Coach Brackett takes his own son off the front line so that Cody can take his place, Cody has to decide what's more important—taking his time to shine, or sticking up for a friend.

Home Ice
By Beatrice Vandervelde

Determined not to miss the hockey season while staying with relatives in Toronto, Tori signs up to play with the Rangers—the worst team in the league. The only girl on her team, she soon befriends Mary, a girl on a rival team who doesn't think much of hockey. At first, Tori's teammates resent her alliance with the enemy—especially Larry, the Rangers' big, loud first-line centre. But when the team discovers her talent for coaching, things start to look up.

Icebreaker
By Steven Barwin

Greg Stokes can tell you exactly when his life took a turn for the worse. It was the day he and his new stepsister, Amy, joined the same hockey team. Like it wasn't bad enough sharing a house, school, and friends—now they're playing on the same line! Before long, the stepsiblings' game is affected by the deep chill between them. Can they thaw their icy relationship for the sake of the team and their new family?